Write yours

How to use writing to help [   ]al pain

ACKNOWLEDGEMENTS

My thanks go to the following:

Rabbi Lionel Blue, for permission to quote from *A Backdoor to Heaven*, published by Darton, Longman and Todd, (© Rabbi Lionel Blue 1979, 1985 and 1994).

The estate of J. B. Priestley, for permission to quote from *The Good Companions*, (© J. B. Priestley 1929 by permission of Peters, Fraser and Dunlop on behalf of the estate of J. B. Priestley).

Tulku Thondup, for permission to quote from *The Healing Power of the Mind*, foreward by Daniel Goleman published by Penguin General 1997, (© Tulku Thondup 1997).

Aber publishing

Books to Improve Your Life

Write yourself well

How to use writing to help heal emotional and physical pain

Ann Coffey

www.aber-publishing.co.uk

© 2008 by Ann Coffey

ISBN: 978-184285-057-2

First published in 2008 by Aber Publishing.
PO Box 225, Abergele, LL18 9AY, United Kingdom.

Website: http://www.aber-publishing.co.uk

Typeset by Vikatan Publishing Solutions, Chennai, India
Printed and bound in Europe
Aber Publishing is a division of Studymates Limited

Contents

Introduction

I began writing in 1972 as part of my treatment after giving birth by caesarean section, going into a coma, and emerging three days later with total amnesia. By then, psychotherapy had already recognised what a useful tool writing could be to help with healing. Other art forms, such as music, painting and sculpture can have the same effect, helping you to:

- express deep emotions,
- change your outlook on the world, or re-assess your worst experiences and
- use them to create something positive.

In my case, the slow process of mending a broken memory bank began with jotting down anything at all I could remember from the past and then using my notes to talk about it with my psychotherapist. She suggested poetry, as a format, to express myself when emotions proved difficult to cope with – (and as I have learned as a teacher), many people who have suffered trauma or bereavement turn to poetry, either to read or to write it, as a natural outlet.

Poetry quickly became a way of life for me. For others, the keeping of a diary serves much the same purpose, or turning your experiences into fiction: simply getting it down on paper can alter the way you look at problems. The page can be a dear friend, a father confessor, your conscience, a comforter: a problem shared is a problem halved.

This book discusses ideas at the beginning of each chapter, and includes checklists and questionnaires. There are writing exercises throughout if you wish to use them, and each chapter concludes with a Writing Assignment to help prompt more on-going, long-term writing. Chapter nine expands on this, and chapter ten offers hypothetical case studies.

As we proceed on this journey of self-discovery together, you should always remember that life is a process of discovery. We learn about the world around us and about our own being. When you have self-doubt, and I am sure that you do, then I urge you to enjoy the moment. Revel in it, wallow like a hippo in mud and rejoice, because it means you are human. At some point in life, all sane people will have self doubt, so enjoy the realisation that you are sane and most of all, you are human.

Ann Coffey

1 Writing as therapy

WRITING HAS BEEN PERFORMING THE ROLE of a therapy for centuries, but only in the last decade or two has it acquired the official description of being 'therapeutic'. For a Victorian housewife alone all day – prior to the invention of the telephone – writing a letter to friend or family was a lifeline: a way to communicate thoughts and feelings and receive some sort of response, albeit delayed. Simply having someone out there who was going to read – or 'listen to' – what you had to say on paper could prove an enormous comfort.

Keeping a diary or journal, with daily input both recording the pleasures and downloading the stresses of everyday life, provided many people with a way of putting emotions into words. This meant they could then take a step back, re-read their writing, and perhaps gain insight into their current life. A diary could fulfil the role of confidante when there was no one to talk to, to whom one could confess intimate thoughts or pour out one's troubles. In the case of letter-writing you were liable to get an opinion back – perhaps not always the one you wanted – but at least the time delay in receiving the response meant you could reflect on what was said, rather than have an argument face to face or over the telephone. The diary would always be a best friend that didn't answer back, but let you come to your own decisions. In both cases, the page was, and still is, an excellent listener.

However, as the Post Office will tell you, personal letter writing is very much on the decline, along with business letters sent via the post. A new generation has come along brought up on email and texting. Actually putting pen to paper, to say what you feel, is far too time-consuming for many. But a piece of paper exiting from a machine is open to view by anyone who happens to be passing – it doesn't have the intimacy of that discreet envelope addressed for one person's eyes only. And a telephone conversation can often be overheard.

So many people are now trying to find a way back to expressing themselves in writing, to replace the natural therapeutic methods lost in this electronic age, while using the tools it has given us. People, today, like to have everything 'chunked' or time-slotted to be able to fit an activity in to their lifestyle. Speed is vital, and the chances are that writing today may well be done straight on to a computer screen rather than using pen and paper. Your age and inclination may determine whether you feel capable of thinking straight on to a machine. What any of us can do, though, is jot down ideas as they occur, using pad and pen wherever we happen to be. That will only take a minute or two, and will be a spontaneous record of how we're feeling and thinking at the time. You can then come back to it and allow yourself more thought about choice of words, sentence structure, and saying what you want to say when you've the time and inclination.

Precedents in therapeutic writing

Medical, psychiatric and social work professions have long understood that for those of us who have difficulty communicating face-to-face, writing can provide an effective outlet. Since the year 2000, the number of Writers-in-Residence has multiplied to boldly take writing into new areas: prisons, mental institutions, hospitals, special schools, women's refuges, old people's homes. The purpose of using writing as a form of therapy in such places will depend on the group being dealt with, but could be any one of the following, or a combination of more than one:

- Self-expression and self-discovery,
- Self-analysis and evaluation of one's life,
- To aid healing through understanding,
- As part of bereavement counselling,
- To relieve emotional stress,
- To smooth over life changes,
- To treat trauma and depression,
- To relieve boredom.

The last of these applies to long-stay hospital patients (especially children, the disabled or anyone confined at home).

Most of what we know about the success or otherwise of writing as therapy has come from group or one-to-one work under the circumstances outlined above. Although the individuals concerned probably wouldn't class their writing as 'therapy', several of those I've encountered through my own creative writing teaching in adult education classes and workshops have been assisted in very similar ways to those methods employed in hospitals, prisons, etc. People will attend a writing group after bereavement, for instance, perhaps having already found out on their own how soothing it could be to "get it down on paper", and now wanting to take this further amongst a like-minded group. And my *Writing Your Life Story* class at Liverpool University always attracted elderly people, sometimes accompanied, wanting to reminisce on paper while there was still time – and delighted that someone was interested enough to listen and encourage. The resulting increase in self-esteem and a sense of purpose that there was some important writing to be done, a life to be recorded, was obvious. Very often there was a life-time's diaries from which to work, usually confined to the women, whereas the men would turn up with crystal-clear memories stored as if on a computer!

So what has the experience of those already working in the area of this type of writing taught us? Certain themes and findings keep recurring if we read their reports (these are not in any particular order of importance):

1. *Concentration Span*: a real problem for the physically or mentally weakened. As Pete Morgan found in his placement as Writer-in-Residence for 6 months at Whittingham Hospital, (a large psychiatric hospital in Preston, Lancashire): "Twenty minutes was fine but any longer than that and the minds began to wander." A similar time-span was found necessary by Phil Emery, who in 1994 set up a pilot project with elderly long-stay patients in Cheadle Hospital in North Staffordshire. The same would apply to writing with children in hospital. So the ensuing target is to find projects and writing exercises that can be done within such a short time-span (see Chapter 9). If you're writing on your own at home, don't expect too much of yourself: take it in steps, perhaps 20 minutes at a time to start with, then build up your concentration span as you build up your writing. You can always leave it and come back to it.

2. *Illiteracy*: anyone can do *some* sort of writing. If a person is handicapped either physically – and unable to hold a pen or tap on

a lap-top computer – or due to severe dyslexia or simply lack of schooling, there is always the possibility of either dictating on to a machine, or using a 'scribe'. A scribe is someone who will do the actual writing for you. You may want to dictate person-to-person, which has the advantage of someone being able to read straight back to you what's just been written so you can hear how it sounds; or if you don't want to involve another person, use a dictating machine.

So why bother with the writing part – why not just talk to your scribe? Because writing provides a record of thoughts, ideas and emotions to which you can return, again and again if need be, to remember how you felt at the time and what's changed since: what did you do to change it? Did having it written down help? In other words, you can *see* what you're thinking: your thoughts don't disappear into thin air.

But probably the most inhibiting factor in preventing someone from using writing as therapy, is confidence. "Oh, I couldn't possibly write like that" is a disclaimer I've often heard – to which the answer is "You don't have to". The first purpose of therapeutic writing is for *you* to see or hear what you've written – no one else. All you have to do initially is make sure you can understand your own writing and thus remember what you were trying to say. If you find writing useful and helpful, and then decide you want to share it with anyone else, some editing may be necessary and you may feel you need help with this for things like grammar and spelling – simply to aid communication. We can all jot down notes to ourselves in some shape or form, and even notes can be the start of something much bigger, as we shall see!

3. *Sharing One's Thoughts*: even if you start out "talking to yourself on paper", you may find this isn't enough. Those who come to creative writing classes of all kinds, and even experienced professional writers, are usually keen for some sort of feedback. The inexperienced writer has a tendency to want to know "Is it any good?" Hidden within that question are several others: "Am I wasting my time?" "How do I compare with other writers?" "Was my writing boring/interesting/hilarious/flat/cliché-ridden?" etc. For writing to be therapeutic, we have to clear our minds of such questions and stop making comparisons. You aren't writing your

thoughts down on paper in order to be compared with any other writers – concentrate on how useful it's being for *you*. If it helps gain insight and confidence, try and explain why, as you write: any reader will find the process interesting, for the same reasons as we read autobiographies and biographies. Understanding *how* the finished product ended up as it did is always as fascinating as the product itself.

In a therapeutic group situation, sharing one's thoughts takes on the added dimension of doing so out loud, there and then, either by discussion of what you're intending to write/have written, or by actually reading out loud. As all those present are there for the same purpose, one thing that group organisers in the past have found is the necessity to establish an understanding from the beginning that no one can be secretive, so that a very open atmosphere results. People need to be very supportive when someone is struggling to express their deepest thoughts and feelings.

Those working in the area of mental health report finding that joint group projects rarely worked. Apart from concentration span problems, actually getting everyone to contribute to a common subject proved difficult. Far more useful was one-to-one work with individuals where writing could be tailored to meet specific needs. However, in the case of the elderly, discussion in a reminiscence group tends to produce a far better common base from which to work – a 'memory-bank' of shared thoughts can produce a whole range of themes to use as the basis for writing sessions.

4. *Discussion*: this has been found to be vital to "get things moving" – to break down barriers, jog memories, relieve inhibitions in a group situation or when writing with one-to-one help. The equivalent for the lone writer is reading and/or note-taking. In both cases, thinking *round* a subject, trying to look at it from an alternative viewpoint, or even trying to look at yourself from an alternative viewpoint, should throw light on the aspect under discussion.

Equally important for those participating is the discovery that they 'aren't the only one', that others out there have been through very similar experiences, and that if you do share your writing they will understand the emotions you're describing. This leads to more confidence from the outset in the idea of writing it down.

5. *Time and Place*: where and when writing is done can for many people mean the difference between success and failure. Any writers' group should think carefully about its writing environment: not only is it imperative to feel comfortable in the presence of one's fellow-writers, but you will need to feel physically comfortable in order not to be distracted from creativity. Talking to professional writers, you often find they have their own personal "cubby-hole", desk, a particular chair or whatever, where they prefer to write. Running writers' groups and classes, I have found that people choose a seat and keep coming back to it, week after week, even though there's no rule which says they always have to sit there. Familiarity with the view from that chair, perhaps? A safe seat?

The same applies to a *time of day:* again, professional writers who may have an enormous output of writing will very often prefer a long morning session, starting early if they're early risers; or write late into the night once inspiration has struck. Individual writers have the choice of what time of day they are at their best, when the brain is freshest. But for those in a hospital or prison situation, writing time may have to fit in to an overall regime timetable. In both these cases, it has been found that the quietest time of day was the best for writing to be achieved, when the bustle and clamour was at its lowest. And on a ward or even in a day-room there were often too many distractions to concentration, whatever the time of day. So one essential basic necessity which you will need to sort out for yourself, is that particular place and time where you feel able to concentrate and get on without interruption.

Genre: for many writers-in-residence dealing with people with short concentration span, poetry was found to be more useful than prose. Even a short story requires more effort than the writing of a haiku, for instance. What you can use to get prose writing started, however, is the recording of incidents and anecdotes – the sort of thing that anyone might enter in their diary. These can then be expanded later to form the backbone of a short story. If writing in the first person is a bit 'too close to home', the incident or anecdote can be applied to a 'he' or a 'she' without further specification.

The lighter verse-forms, such as rhyming couplets, can be built up from week to week to form a longer poem. Or try humour – a limerick is only 5 lines. And one other area that has been proved to work is the use of *writing games* – short, sweet and should provide a laugh. See the end of this chapter for writing game ideas. They can provide a light-hearted way in to writing, getting someone used to the idea of communicating via words without the notion of it being formal and compulsory – with all the memories of school which that may conjure up.

Simply 'messing about' with words can provide a new-found freedom: examining rhyme, onomatopoeia, and repetition in poetry examples, for instance, and then having a go oneself; toying and tinkering to come up with newly-invented words to use in nonsense poetry; thinking up a selection of palindromes; or exploring sound-patterns in the English language.

6. *Production*: another recurring emphasis arising from past experiences in therapeutic writing was that at the end there should be a final product – something visible and tangible achieved, typed up and recorded that could be seen or heard – a reminder for people to come back to, that writing things down can produce the goods.

Exercises

(a) *The Fruit Game*: first, think of a well-known person. This could be a film-star, politician, football star, singer, TV star. If that person were an item of fruit or a vegetable, what would they be? Is there anyone you can think of who has always reminded you of such an item? What is it about their appearance, voice or mannerisms that causes you to make that association? (e.g. shape, skin-tone, hair-style) Now compose at least one simile and one metaphor applied to that person, e.g. *simile:* Joe Bloggs is as skinny as a stick of rhubarb; Mrs. Bloggs always looks like a squashed plum.

Metaphor: Tommy Bloggs is a real gooseberry when it comes to girls; Julie Bloggs is the apple of her dad's eye.

Now can you use your simile and metaphor in a short poem? A Haiku is a Japanese verse form of 3 lines made up of 17 syllables, divided 5, 7, 5 and doesn't need to rhyme. Try a haiku – e.g.:

> *"Once, Sir Cyril Smith*
> *Got kissed by Margaret Thatcher.*
> *Now he's a pumpkin."*

(b) *The Furniture Game*: now do the same as you did for the Fruit Game, associating someone with a piece of furniture. But this time you might like to either write a poem, or begin a short story with a piece of dialogue between you and that item of furniture, e.g. you've just plonked yourself down into a comfy chair, and a voice complains about being sat on; or you've slammed a wardrobe door shut and it immediately comes open again, just to annoy you! Write the ensuing discussion/argument.

(c) *Use of Objects*: you can adapt either of the above writing games for a group situation. Members take in a variety of fruit and place them where everyone can see them. Each person then takes one item and describes its appearance, touch, what it tastes like (whether or not they actually eat it at the time!), and how they feel about it (love it or hate it). Are there memories associated with eating that particular fruit? Or if few fruits are in season, cut up several small pieces of card, write a different item of fruit on each one, then pop them in a container for each person to 'pick one out of the hat'. They then have to describe the fruit using simile and metaphor without actually mentioning its name. After the description has been written (either in prose or poetry), each person reads it out and the rest have to guess what fruit is being described. This group exercise can be applied to a variety of miscellaneous objects. The main point is to get used to describing something without having it sound like a dictionary definition or part of a scientific thesis.

Assignment 1

Start now to keep a Learning Diary. Record your thoughts and reactions as you read through this book: do you agree or disagree with ideas? Has your own experience been the same as, or the opposite of, other people's? How do you feel about the exercises – too easy/difficult?

At this stage we merely need diary-style jottings. Later you may want to do a complete write-up and turn your jottings into a review of your progress.

2 **Reasons for writing**

TODAY THERE ARE MANY DIFFERENT TYPES of therapy – psychotherapy, art therapy, aromatherapy, hypnotherapy, behaviour therapy, etc. – that can either be used on their own or in conjunction with one or more others. Writing, too, can be used with any of the other therapy forms. It provides a tool for expression and description when used in conjunction, and on its own the listening page may be all that's needed to make someone feel better. By clarifying our feelings and thoughts sufficiently to get them down on paper, we have already gone part of the way towards untangling how we think and feel. Writing as therapy leaves the writer in total control of their own therapy: no one is going to urge you to write if inspiration isn't there, you only write what *you* want, and in a group situation only discuss what you want to discuss.

Diagnosis

Before we can begin to feel better, we usually need a diagnosis to tell us what's wrong. You may have suffered illness or bereavement, for instance, and be aware of what that has done to your life, so the diagnosis is in place and writing may be one of several attempts at therapy. On the other hand, occasionally people discover something helps them to feel better without having been aware of exactly what was wrong. Therapy may not have been prescribed or anticipated – but if something comes along that offers relief, you will want more of it.

If the reason for taking up writing is because you know it has helped others who have suffered the same trauma as yourself, why not move straight to a writing group? There, you'll have the support of people wanting to write for the same reasons as you. In much the same way as Alcoholics Anonymous or Weightwatchers work to help people, the companionship of a group can prove as beneficial as the activity of writing itself. You discuss the same problems about the difficulties of writing it down, and listen to what others have to say; in return you're expected to contribute at some point – perhaps not until you're familiar with the group. This may put some people off the idea of a writing group.

If you're on your own trying to find a way into writing, start by asking yourself a few questions about why you want to write, and build up to a self-diagnosis.

Questionnaire

1. Do you feel the *need to communicate* with other people, but are not in a position to do so due to physical, mental or social handicap?
2. How do you *feel about writing*: confident? Unsure? Afraid? (and if so, why?)
3. Do you feel happier *talking to people* than writing?
4. Are you worried about *exploring your past* in writing? Can you say why?
5. Are you an *introvert or an extrovert*? (Inward-looking or outgoing?)
6. Are you worried about *who might see or hear* what you've written?
7. Are you confident that writing *might help you*, if you could get started?
8. Do you know *what sort of writing* you want to do? Poetry/ fiction/non-fiction/script-writing?
9. What do you *enjoy reading* most? Have you one particular author or poet about whom you've always thought "I'd like to write like that"?
10. How do you feel about the idea of *joining a therapeutic writing group*? Can you envisage ever feeling ready to do so?

Begin by jotting down brief answers to the above to start with, just a word or two. The main thing is to do some thinking. Now expand each answer into a whole sentence. The questions aren't in any particular order, so you may want to re-arrange them to make the whole piece coherent, and perhaps join up shorter answers to make a longer sentence. For example, if your answer to no. 4 was 'yes' and to no. 6 was also 'yes', your sentence could well read: "The only reason I'm worried about exploring my past in writing is because I don't want to hurt my parents, should they read what I've written."

This 'diagnosis' is for your eyes only, to help you have clear in your mind why you want to write and how it might help you. Keep it and add more thoughts and ideas to it as you progress with your writing: see if your attitude to writing changes. Use it as a starting point for the time being.

Palliative treatment or cure?

A 'palliative' treatment is one that lessens pain or gives temporary relief. What writing things down can't do is provide a solution to problems: you still have to manage that elsewhere. In that respect, writing is a palliative treatment that can offer understanding and a means of letting go of withheld feelings and emotions. It can remain totally private – unless you want to edit what you've jotted down for anyone else to read. And you can record how you feel 'on the spot' as it happens, your reactions to people and situations, without upsetting anyone – and do an analysis later to try and understand why you reacted the way you did.

Writing will not cure serious mental health problems on its own, and for a proportion of society for whom writing is an alien concept, and for whom one of the longest things they ever write is a note for the milkman, 'getting it down on paper' may not be an option. But for many, simply discovering how good it feels to have told someone – even if you're talking to yourself on paper – can be a major turnaround in a struggle with life. Writing can be a one-to-one with yourself: ask yourself why you did something; summarise the options to yourself; conduct an interview with yourself to help you analyse what makes you tick!

Being honest with yourself

"Truth I learnt in seminaries, honesty I learnt elsewhere … slowly, I began to suspect I had other teachers, too close for comfort, whom I had never honoured enough or listened to enough … my own mistakes, the best teachers a man has ever had." (Rabbi Lionel Blue in his autobiography, *A Backdoor to Heaven*).

Pain, grief, insecurity, confusion, even memory loss, may mean that when you do start to write you feel unable to disclose everything on the page. You might have spent a long time trying to bury painful memories – but they may still be nagging. Don't let this put you off making a start – there are ways round it (see No. 6 below). But be aware of the 'clutter' that you bring along with you, which may fog up what you want to say and cause frustration:

1. *Preconceived Ideas*: you may have preconceived ideas of what writing is about: something literary types do, not for the likes of you? Something that needs a wide vocabulary, good grammar and spelling? Is 'proper' writing something you left behind in school? Well lose these ideas! Lose your inhibitions about spelling, etc. and concentrate on the flow of ideas and thoughts using jottings. Get used to the idea of taking it in stages, and this is only the first tentative step – the 50 kilometre walk is for professionals!

2. *Prejudices and Resentments*: some of these may be subconscious, but even if you're aware that you're prejudiced against someone or something, be prepared to admit it to yourself on the page. In fact, have a thoroughly good moan about it, get it off your chest – then make the effort to try and look at it from the opposing viewpoint.

3. *Entrenched Beliefs*: one way you can use writing is for some private soul-searching. In discussion with other people you may feel unable to question, to challenge what you and they have always accepted other people's reactions may be shock, disappointment, or disgust that you should even conceive of questioning the status quo. To help you sort yourself out, weigh up pros and cons on the page – make lists 'For' and 'Against' if that helps – to let you at least know *why* you think that way or have acted that way (and why others hold their beliefs and behave the way they do, too).

4. *How do You Feel About Yourself*? – Lionel Blue again, following a breakdown: "Until my analysis I had never dared to tackle this problem because I had never liked myself." So he decided to give a party in his imagination – and invite the various bits of himself to it, so they could learn to put up with each other. "There was my mind, my soul and my body, and a meeting was arranged."

He describes the resulting mental gathering as "uncomfortable", but gives himself a pat on the back for having managed it at all!

And how do you feel about *yourself*? Are there bits of you that you're not too sure about? Are you confident enough in your own abilities, and that your ideas and beliefs will stand up to scrutiny, to be perfectly open with other people? Or do you spend a lot of the time saying to yourself "No one will listen to what I have to say because I'm too stupid/ugly/clumsy/insignificant?" Well, a page will listen to what you have to say: get used to asserting yourself, your opinions and your beliefs in writing, and you'll be surprised how having managed to write it all clearly will help you to *say* it all clearly.

5. *Self disclosure*: unless we are prepared to disclose our thoughts and feelings to others, they will not be able to understand our current position. Try answering the following questions honestly:

- Are you kidding yourself (as well as others)?
- Has the real you – that brightly shining gem of a person – been hidden from view all these years?
- Have you been trying to present an image to the world when inside you were an earthquake waiting to happen?
- Have you found it difficult to be honest with other people?
- Do you continually feel suspicious of other people's honesty?
- Under what circumstances would you feel lying was justified? Can you say why? Make a list.
- Can you remember any occasions when you've not been honest with other people or yourself, and have since regretted it?
- When you have been honest with other people, what has been their response? Was honesty always the best policy – or a waste of time?

6. *Options When Starting to Write*: if you don't feel up to self-disclosing on the page just yet, but want to make some sort of start – to show willing to yourself – try:

- *Anonymity*: that well-known 'Aggrieved' person of Tunbridge Wells, or 'angry of Cardiff', doesn't have a name or a face … but certainly has an opinion! When newspapers or magazines ask readers for their opinions, write your thoughts as if you were going to send them in – you can actually do so, but the main point is to get used to putting them in writing. Even when their writing is well developed, many writers still prefer to use a pseudonym. They can have their say without recriminations, and the private persona can remain private. Only when they pick up a pen do they also change metaphorical hats, and wear their 'writer's hat'.

- *Generalising*: in discussion both on and off the page, rather than use the first person 'I' throughout, you can contribute to an argument by generalising, e.g. "Don't you think society's opinions nowadays are ...?" or "I've heard people say ...". If you're worried that you're a minority of one, and have found it difficult to speak up for fear of ridicule or because you feel ignorant and suspect the rest of the world will know better, introducing your opinions in this way should at the very least make others consider a different viewpoint. In return, you'll have to do the same – which may make you think again and reform your opinions, but could lead to them being strengthened.

Confessions

The Reader's Encyclopedia defines Confessions as a literary genre as follows: "A form of auto-biography or simulated autobiography. Intimate and possibly guilty matters not usually disclosed are 'confessed', presumably to serve some sort of didactic purpose."

Confessions constitute a literary genre that began with the *Confessions of St. Augustine* (397–401), a spiritual autobiography designed to show details of the soul's progress, the first work in literature to be concerned entirely with an introspective analysis of the author's own spiritual and emotional experiences. Among the most famous confessions in literature are Thomas de Quincey's *Confessions of an English Opium Eater* (1822). De Quincey was an essayist and critic, who lived from 1785–1859, and this largely autobiographical account of his early life describes the growth and effects of his habit of taking opium. The Confessions cover his childhood and schooling, his absconding from Manchester Grammar School at the age of 16, and his wanderings in North Wales and London. Later, as a student at Oxford, he began taking opium, which became a life-long addiction. His writing was often jotted down quickly in odd places – De Quincey was deeply in debt and life was hardly easy.

But the final product reads much better than you might expect of random jottings from someone under the influence of opium. This is despite the writer's claim that he wrote "… to think aloud, and follow my own humours (rather) than much to consider who is listening to me". A sense of audience is something that a writer acquires from practice at talking to *other* people on paper, and writing so that they may understand. Confessions, as a genre, are aimed at talking to *oneself* on paper, for all the reasons discussed so far in this chapter. There will be a lot of autobiographical narrative involved as a basic structure, but there should also be a strong element of interpretation of what those experiences meant at the time, the effect they had, and how you now interpret them, years on, with hindsight.

So Confessions will need to be *selective* autobiography: cut out the details that don't bear directly on character formation and the development of how you think and feel. Thomas de Quincey's Confessions contain many admissions of personal failure – that 'being honest' with oneself – but there is a wry smile coming through the words a lot of the time. Where he does perhaps waver a little in his honesty is with regard to his opium habit: he repeatedly denies that his drug habit has been a 'culpable self-indulgence' … but goes to the trouble of thinking out the excuses he *would* make for himself, if there were indeed any guilt involved!

And Confessions don't have to be exact in time-sequence or chronology, but rather can be based on particular areas such as the stress of modern living; childhood innocence; hopes and dreams. Each area can then be covered either working backwards from a present-day effect to discuss the probable cause, or vice versa. Thomas de Quincey, for instance, moves back and forth from topic to topic and appears to go off at a tangent in what, from any other writer, might well have been a confused maze (these started out, after all, as random jottings). There does, however, have to be some editing somewhere to make 'jottings' readable and maintain a connecting thread.

The reason he gives for writing his Confessions, in his address "To the Reader" at the beginning, is a wish to be;

"useful and instructive … and that must be my apology for breaking through that delicate and honourable reserve, which, for the most part, restrains us from the public exposure of our own errors and infirmities. Nothing, indeed, is more revolting to English feelings than the spectacle of a human being obtruding on our notice his moral ulcers or scars, and tearing away that 'decent drapery' which time, or indulgence to human frailty, may have drawn over them."

He makes this his excuse for hesitating "about the propriety of allowing this, or any part of my narrative, to come before the public eye, until after my death" – but then gives his reasons for deciding to go ahead. "Guilt and misery shrink … from public notice: they court privacy and solitude; and, … (in the affecting language of Mr. Wordsworth)

"Humbly to express
A penitential loneliness"

From: *The White Doe of Rylstone*

That "humbly to express/A penitential loneliness" can well translate as the need to air something that is troubling you, because you're feeling sorry for yourself or lonely.

Asserting yourself

Are you one of those people to whom things happen, rather than who makes things happen? When you're in the minority, do you stick to your views or kowtow to the majority? Are you always happy to let others make the decisions?

The concept of Assertiveness Training now pervades management and training schemes everywhere. It came about as a behaviour therapy technique in the mid-1970s, when people were encouraged to stand up for their own personal rights without treading on other people's toes. This means expressing yourself directly and honestly. However, when this is applied to writing, once we do decide to let the world read or listen to what we've written, it is essential to edit out all our non-assertive moans and groans as well as any aggressive accusations. A confessional diary form, for instance, will allow you to say what you feel and think *for your eyes only*. Once it is public, a sense of audience comes into play.

Assertiveness means learning to choose how you want to behave, or what you want to say or write, in certain situations without the inhibiting factors of fear of others' reactions, and fear of rejection or anger. For that to happen, a little tact should be lightly applied, along with some forethought as to whether what you've written will do unnecessary damage, hurt someone, or infringe their rights in some way (e.g. their right to privacy). Getting it off *your* chest may mean dumping it firmly on someone else's.

So if you are going to name names and reveal your true feelings in writing that you intend to make public in some way – even if it's to others close to you or during group therapy sessions – ask yourself the following questions first:

- Am I being fair, and conceding that the other side may have a point, or blindly over-reacting?
- How will those reading this react? Have I made myself clear? – think round all possible interpretations. Can I say it a little more tactfully, while still remaining true to what I believe?
- On the other hand, have I told it like it is/was? Or am I being *too* tactful?
- Have I maintained throughout "I'm right, everyone else is wrong, end of argument"? Or have I conceded that occasionally I may be wrong?
- Have I *demanded* a fair hearing … or *asked* for one? (aggression demands; assertiveness asks)
- Am I prepared to be criticised on this or any other aspects of my life? If such-and-such a criticism were levelled at me, how would I react?
- Do I really *need* people to like me? If they don't, isn't it their hard luck?

Now see Exercise (b) below for a follow-up exercise using your answers to these questions. If you're feeling extremely angry, resentful, or sorry for yourself, you'll find it difficult to be assertive: emotions will get in the way. But in order to deal constructively with problems and clarify thoughts, we need to do some cool analysis. By all means, go for it, have a huff and a puff on the page to yourself – then in order to really help yourself, move on to take control of your reactions and understand them. One way to go about this is to assert yourself on the page.

Exercises

(a) *Self-disclosure*: have a look at your answers to No.5 under "Self Disclosure" earlier in this chapter. This material can form the basis of a short article or 'think-piece' (as the world of journalism describes an article for a newspaper or magazine that deals with a serious topic designed to make the reader think, as opposed to straightforward factual news reporting). Initially, you may have answered these questions with a single word or phrase; now elaborate on each of them. For instance, you may have qualms about answering with a plain 'yes' or 'no' – there may be quite a few ifs and buts involved. Think about them and deal with each item in turn:

1. Make notes on anything else that comes to mind such as examples or anecdotes from real life, either your own experience or things you've heard about, and your reservations about your initial answers.
2. Decide if you want to name names and quote people, or generalise.
3. Include your reactions as you write.
4. Consider your reader: the analysis we did following the questionnaire, at the beginning of this chapter, was for your eyes only. Now assume that you're relating your thoughts to a particular 'audience' – friends, relatives, a group to which you belong, for instance. Choose one set of people, and think what you'd now put in by way of explanation for them, and what you'd leave out – and why this sort of editing might be necessary (e.g. to avoid hurting someone).

Using your notes, do a write-up disclosing just as much as you feel capable of.

(b) *Asserting Yourself*: using the seven questions asked in this section earlier, write a critical assessment either of exercise (a) above, or any other piece of writing you've already done. Decide if you've been fair concerning other people – and then tell yourself the answer. If you've not written anything yet, have a look in newspapers and magazines for an article where someone is making a case or offering an argument, giving firm opinions, and apply these seven questions to the article. Your assessment may be as short as seven sentences or as long as seven paragraphs, but should criticise the writer's thinking both positively as well as negatively: if you agree and the idea's been well-expressed, say so; if you disagree and think there isn't a shred of evidence, say so.

Assignment 2: "How do I love thee? Let me count the ways"

One positive reason for writing is to celebrate all the good things you have going for you. The title for this assignment is the first line from Sonnet 43 in *Sonnets from the Portuguese* by Elizabeth Barrett Browning (1806–1861). She was referring to her love for her husband, but for this assignment the idea is to apply the question to oneself, and come up with a list. Try assessing your strengths:

- What do other people like about you?
- What do you do really well?
- What are you pleased that you can do/can't do?
- Any examples of you caring for others; acting assertively; thinking positively?
- What do people always count on you for, with justification?
- What have you the guts to do/the diplomacy not to do?

Now write a celebration of yourself. Assume you're selling yourself in a job interview – and let your ego have a real boost!

3   Creativity and lateral thinking

The creative process

IN 1958, BASIC BOOKS OF NEW YORK published *Human Potentialities* by Gardner Murphy, in which he divided the creative process into 4 stages:

- immersion,
- consolidation,
- illumination and
- verification.

Borrowing his headings, we can explain the creative process as follows:

1. *Immersion*: This means becoming totally familiar with all aspects of your topic. It could take the form of reading widely and making notes, for instance, or in the case of life-story writing, digging out those old letters, photos, mementoes, and dredging the memory bank for remembered characters, tales, anecdotes, incidents. If personal memories are painful, try exploring the data available about what else was going on at the time – are you perhaps one of many who suffered in the same way (e.g. during war-time)? Immerse yourself in facts and figures about social conditions in order to put your own experiences into perspective. If you were writing a biography – someone else's life story – you'd need to do exactly the same. In the case of a novel, the 'Immersion' would constitute all necessary research prior to actually doing any writing (for a historical novel, this would involve becoming totally familiar with a particular period; for a crime novel, swotting up on the law and police procedures).

2. *Consolidation (or Incubation)*: The serious thinking part. This involves asking "what if this had happened instead of that?" and choosing what to concentrate on and what you don't need to include: what has creative potential and what will surely be a dead

end? A lot of the data gathered in Stage (1) may not have sunk in consciously: you will have gained impressions and feelings or reacted emotionally without doing so deliberately. Intuition and insight will be generated at this stage – daylight may slowly dawn as a result of pondering problems, recognising patterns and making connections that hadn't previously occurred to you. This is where lateral thinking is vital (see below).

3. *Illumination*: That flash of inspiration in your thinking! During Stages (1) and (2) you will have been charging the battery ready for the creative spark that now happens. Up till now your research and thinking may well have followed the same path as others before you; now your own original ideas are generated.

4. *Verification*: Not all bright ideas prove to be any use. Now comes the test: can you use your inspiration? Can it be adapted for practical purposes? So you've discovered gravity – so what? In the case of writing for healing purposes, verification might take the form of inventing a third person (hero or heroine) to use for a short story, novel, or TV script to demonstrate your own or someone else's life experiences. Or coming up with an alternative time and place in which to set your tale, having done some historical research and discovered similarities between, say, Victorian England and now. In short, can you now find a suitable vehicle for you to express your idea? And will it work?

Lateral thinking

It was Edward de Bono, in 1969, who came up with the distinction between 'vertical' and 'lateral' thinking. Vertical thinking moves logically from A to B to C in a straight explicable line; lateral thinking makes sideways leaps, sometimes of quantum proportions: what you might call alternative thinking. This could involve adopting a viewpoint no one has considered before – the dragon's opinion of St. George, (from the legend where St. George supposedly slays a dragon), for instance – and turning accepted ideas on their heads. The result will certainly be different, but won't be of much use unless it produces insights, explanations or inspiration to you, the writer, or to other people.

It's a very useful tool for therapeutic writing, not only to generate ideas, but also to allow you to challenge the way you've always thought – and perhaps not dared to consider alternatives. Have you become set in your linear, vertical ways of thinking? Try taking a sideways step, abandon logic and transgress a few limits.

Neither vertical nor lateral thinking should, however, be used exclusive of the other. You will need both for your creativity. Try thinking in a straight line, then make comparisons: compare and contrast people, situations, incidents, all the time asking "why?" Can you recognise similarities anywhere between totally different areas of life? Perhaps a new and unexpected connection that no one else has made before? This is how many break-throughs in science, engineering and the arts came about – someone adapting a theory from one area of learning to solve a problem in a different context. In order to acquire the knowledge in the first place, vertical thinking and logic will have been used; lateral application of it produces inspired creativity and inventions.

Prompting creativity

Even if you have started out to write carefully following the 4 stages outlined earlier under The Creative Process, there is no guarantee that you won't come to a dead end somewhere, and end up with writer's block, staring at a blank page. So in this section we shall look at the various methods you can use to prompt the mind into action and prod the imagination. The "use it, don't lose it" concept is a therapeutic one – keep that brain active, set yourself a challenge (which can take the form of writing exercises and assignments), read and explore round your chosen area, then indulge in some lateral thinking.

1. As general advice when approaching any writing, don't be afraid to *sleep on it*: either literally, or lay your reading and research data to one side and come back to it. Don't expect to start writing merely because you've had an idea of some sort. Let it mature. Keep thinking about it – think *round* it from all angles rather than launch in. Simply applying the brain elsewhere for a time and coming back to where you were – perhaps re-reading what you've written so far, what you wrote in the past, or re-reading what other people have written on the same topic – may well lead to a new angle occurring to you, or a new connection being made.

2. *When inspiration does strike – be ready*! That means being armed with at least a pen wherever you are – in bed, on the train, wherever. Capture that fleeting bright idea before you forget it. One of mankind's most creative times of day is that grey area between sleep and waking which is often ripe with images and impressions that the fully-conscious mind may not be aware of. So keep a pad and a pen by your bed or your favourite armchair, ready to jot down anything that comes to mind, either as you doze off or when you wake up.

Get used to your own shorthand – it may be necessary to record quickly an impression or an event, or a landscape whizzing past viewed from a train. Those initial jottings can be articulated later into readable prose or poetry.

3. *Visual Stimuli*

   (a) *Use of Objects and Memorabilia* I have already mentioned mementoes and old photos earlier when talking about the 'immersion' process for autobiographical writing. How often do we spot an object – an ornament, a toy, an item of furniture, for instance – and it jogs the memory into remembering something similar to that we grew up with. From there, the memory can go on and follow a whole trail of objects – through a house or a shop, for instance, – to create an impression of times gone by.

   Whether you loved it or hated it, you can use an object or memento to spark off writing, e.g.

   - *Any incidents* you can remember involving this particular item? Relate them.
   - *People* you associate with it: who gave it to you or your household? Or who made it? Describe them.
   - Even if you have no personal memories associated with an object that appeals to you, *what else does it remind you of*? Examine shape, colour, any smell or sound it makes, and try to explain in writing why you make those connections.
   - *Object of desire*? Is there any one particular item you've always wanted to own but have never been able to? An expensive painting, perhaps, or an exclusive piece of jewellery? Describe the item first, then try to explain its appeal.

(b) *One set of items* that you can use as visual stimuli is a *small collection* of anything: are you a collector of old letters or postcards? A stamp collector? Even the contents of a sewing box, knitting bag, tool kit, seed box, button box can be used. Examine the various examples in the collection – remind you of anything? (another single object, perhaps, that was made by someone using this particular type of wool/wood?) A postcard to remind you of a holiday, one particular stamp you found somewhere unexpected? A button saved from a beloved garment that simply wore out, and that you still miss? Or that old packet of seeds, which did so well when planted. Use any of these to record details and impressions – or even to make a written instruction to yourself for the future, e.g. to revisit that place or to have another try with those seeds.

(c) *Pictures, paintings, sculptures and photos generally.* Whether these have close personal connections or not, what they depict can always be used as a stimulus for writing, e.g. try to find one picture, painting, photo or sculpture which *typifies what you most love/hate about the genre*, and study it. Has Picasso completely put you off modern art, for instance? Are you sick of that oriental lady or that fruit bowl/vase of flowers everywhere? Is there one particular cartoonist that you love/hate? What would your ideal photo calendar have for its 12 months of the year? Why? Try to explain, as if to someone who doesn't know you at all, why you prefer one type of painting or drawing to another, or a certain type of photo-subject. *Old photos*: there are many collections in book form of photographs recording the passing of time and social changes, or you may have several photo-albums full in your own archives to draw on. Delve in to see how you respond: there may be a whole era you'd really rather not remember – if so, why? Try to record your response to photos from the past, and ask yourself:

- "Those were the days"? Would you like to relive that decade? What were the features that made it memorable?
- If prior to your own life, would you like to have been alive then, or are you glad you weren't?

25

- Fashions: very often we look back at ourselves dressed in what was fashionable 10, 20, 30 years ago or more, and either deplore our appearances or wish we could go back to then. How did you feel at the time looking like that, and how did you feel about others similarly dressed? Apart from clothes, what else springs to mind (or may well be depicted in an old photo)? E.g. changing tastes in cars, housing or leisure pursuits.

It may help to plan your response to the above ideas if you make a list 'For' and 'Against' before starting to write, and work from this, comparing and contrasting advantages and disadvantages. Even if you come down firmly on one side, deciding this was the ideal time to have lived, or you're jolly glad you weren't alive then, such a list will enable you to present a more balanced argument.

See Exercise (a) at the end of this chapter for using all the notes you've made in this section.

(d) *Visual Descriptions*: there are various tools you can use to help yourself chisel out a readable description of a landscape, a garden, a building or the weather. Both to describe somewhere you've felt at home, happy and relaxed, or somewhere that's left you feeling paranoid, you will need similes, metaphors, onomatopoeia and strong verbs (see glossary definitions). These 4 tools are practical aids for any description where moods, strong emotions, impressions and feelings come into play. Use them to depict colours and sounds, and to paint a picture in words:

- Onomatopoeia is sound echoing sense. If you have been using metaphor to describe someone as a giant of a man, you may well say 'he stomped around', where stomped implies the sound he made with his big weighty feet. The clang of a trolley-bus, the coo of a dove, the lowing of cattle- all these words echo the sound made by the bus/dove/cattle as we pronounce them.
- *Strong verbs*: one way to use onomatopeoia is via strong verbs. A strong verb is one which says far more, all on its

own without a qualifying adverb, than a weak verb, which is vague and needs several more words round it to achieve the picture, e.g.

WEAK	STRONG
She laughed loudly	she cackled
To go slowly	to crawl
He was happy in his new situation	he rejoiced in his new situation

Strong verbs very often go hand-in-hand with metaphors or actually are metaphors themselves. Lots of adjectives and adverbs all over the place have a deadening effect on prose – they delay progress where action is needed and aren't the answer to creating atmosphere. A few may help.

The weather is one whole area about which we British can discourse at length – and it has produced some excellent atmospheric, moody writing! In the same way as what is actually happening outside can leave us feeling physically and mentally depressed, a vivid weather description can help to unload that depression on to the page. Have a good moan about February, or rejoice in June's sunshine:

"The March wind went shrieking over the Midland Plain. Under a sky as rapid, ragged and tumultuous as a revolution, all the standing water, the gathered thaws and rains of February, filling the dykes and spreading over innumerable fields, was ruffled and whitened, so that the day glittered coldly. There was ice even yet in this wind, but already there were other things too, shreds and tatters of sunlight, sudden spicy gusts, distant trumpetings of green armies on the march."

From: *The Good Companions* by J. B. Priestley

Here, we've still got similes, metaphors and onomatopeoia used to help describe wintry weather.

Exercise

Here are some strong verbs to do with the weather. Can you now write about 50 words on the subject of how you feel about rain, including most of them? Try to include at least one simile and one metaphor – and can you find an alternative adjective to describe rain other than 'grey'?

| Ooze | saturate | drizzle | deluge |
| Squelch | wallow | splosh | bucket |

4. *Aural Stimuli*

(a) *Eavesdroppings* are a ready-made source of anecdotes to write about. What you may overhear, or other people may have overheard and then related to you, is real life as it happened – the gossipy version. You can always 'adapt' the true version by altering names, times and places, if you're afraid of hurting someone or being sued. What you should be keeping your ears open for are snippets that pin-point facets of life today, the sort of thing to which your response is "Typical!" or "How awful!" when you hear the details, and which you can then use to instigate a piece of writing explaining your own attitudes or similar experiences. You'll find that the anecdotes that stick in the brain do so because you relate to them in some way: ask yourself why?

Not only do we hear things "over the garden fence" or from the seat behind on the bus or train, but often news programmes on TV or radio finish off with just this type of anecdote – usually a light-hearted occurrence. In the same way as you'd use this type of thing to begin a chat with a neighbour – "Did you hear about …?" – you can use the same item to set yourself off writing and record your reactions. Make a point of having a listen in to children talking; teenagers; old people – and see what topics are typical in their conversations. Don't forget to note down the gems you hear, to use in your writing!

(b) *Media Stories*: use radio, TV and the newspapers to stimulate writing ideas. Heard anything recently that's made you immediately turn off in disgust? Or remain glued until the end of the programme? Whatever prompts your thoughts in this way can be used to clarify your thinking, and set out for yourself how you feel about a topic.

Rather than mutter in annoyance all day so that your colleagues or family have to suffer, or bore someone silly by praising a thing/person effusively – tell it to the page. You can ride a hobby-horse as long as you want in writing – get it off your chest, then if you want to present a more reasoned and less emotional reaction to a particular topic, re-read what you've written and condense your feelings/attitudes/reasoning: try to summarise them in one sentence if possible. Assume you're going to present your ideas or attitudes on radio or TV yourself – you'd need to be succinct, so pick out the most relevant features.

Exercise

"Letter to the Times": Follow any programme on radio or TV that has set you thinking or caused an emotional reaction, and make notes about your response. Now write a letter as if you were going to send it to the Times newspaper letters page making your views clear to the world. If this helps you clarify your thoughts, it could be the first of many – build up to a whole private letters collection (you might even decide to actually post one!)

(c) *Recordings*: Who would you most like a one-to-one with? Someone whose opinions you value may be about to give a talk on radio or TV, or you may discover someone holding forth, either as a deliberate monologue or simply because they were given suffi-cient air-space to have their say. Record this on tape, play it back and have a think, then reply to them in writing. List the questions you'd want to ask them and the replies you'd give to what they had to say. You may not even need to do any recording, if you're able to make notes 'live' as you hear their discourse.

Music has always been a source of inspiration for writers, espe-cially for poets. As sounds conjure up pictures, try describing those pictures in words. Lots of music reflects the surroundings in which it's created – the place (e.g. church music); the people (ethnic music); or the instruments (a brass band). Quality of voice affects the interpreta-tion put on a song or hymn: an African choir in Bulawayo Cathedral can sing the same hymn as an English choir in Canterbury Cathedral and the voices sound very different. This is because of the 'timbre' or quality of sound rather than pitch or volume. Adjectives that spring to mind are ones such as 'stately' music, 'mournful', 'attack-ing' (Tchaikovsky's 1812 Overture?), 'brooding', 'haunting', … what do we mean by 'spooky' music, the sort of thing we hear accompa-nying a horror/ghost film? The term "bring on the violins" we now use to describe a romantic episode on film or TV – why have violins become associated in this way? What is it about their cat-gut sound? And when we call a piece of music a "dirge" we associate it with death and funerals – slow and mournful.

Music can be therapeutic on its own: immerse yourself in your favourite sounds or your favourite singer's voice and let it flow over you. If you want to take it a stage further and add another dimension in writing, try borrowing from the CD library "something entirely different". Ethnic music, such as what you hear in an Indian or Chinese restaurant, or Gaelic panpipes backing a TV documentary on Scotland, can summon to mind immediate images of that part of the world – why? Often the instruments used may be made locally from indigenous materials and their music will have evolved over many centuries. We only need to hear a few notes to know what part of the world we're in.

Exercise

Music and Ceremonies: describe a particular ceremony or occasion with which you associate a piece of music dear to you. This could be anything from a wedding march to a big sporting occasion preceded by singing or band playing. The All-Blacks rugby team against Wales at Cardiff's Millennium Park, perhaps? Try to describe the difference in sounds between the Maori Haka and Mae Hen Wlad Fy Nhadau (Land of my Fathers): both examples of ethnic 'singing', but entirely different (one attacking, the other lyrical – but both aimed at raising spirits).

5. *Use of Quotes: The Penguin Dictionary of Quotations* (ed. J.M. and M.J. Cohen, first published 1960, ISBN 1-85007-022-9) is a rich source of man's sayings to use as a starting-point for a poem or think-piece of prose. Usually, you can borrow a phrase – or even the whole quote if short enough – to use as your title and work from that, e.g. "Men should not work. For men who work cannot dream, and wisdom comes in dreams" (Chief of the Flat Face tribe): an immediate title that presents itself from this quote is *Wisdom Comes in Dreams*. You can add a question-mark (*Wisdom Comes in Dreams?*) if your thesis is one of questioning this statement. Or have you your own personal treasure-trove of quotes on which you rely for your philosophy of life? Tell the

world! Tell us if they've been tested in any way, and how they stood up to experience. Perhaps you have a quote or two that's been handed down in your family – something someone from a previous generation could always be relied on to come out with on a particular occasion (when talking about the weather, for instance? Or describing their marriage partner?)

Exercise

Choose one of the following quotes that strikes you as particularly relevant to your own experience, and write either a poem or a story demonstrating how it works in practice:

"There is no greater grief than to recall a time of happiness when in misery"

Dante

"Rather light a candle than complain about the darkness."

Ancient Chinese proverb

"Turn your face to the sun and the shadows fall behind you."

Maori proverb

You could start by listing what you think makes people happy generally, then move on to what makes you happy personally.

6. *Miscellaneous Ideas*

(a) *Obituaries.* Write your own obituary! Do an assessment – an overview of your life to date – and decide which events, people, places, etc. were of most influence, and *how* you were influenced. What were the resulting achievements/failures you made? You can then choose to do a humorous obituary listing your failures, or simply decide how you'd want to be remembered after your death. Or do the 'alternative' version: instruct those reading your obituary why they should make every effort to forget you.

Or write a short obituary for someone else: this could be someone you miss terribly, or someone you're thoroughly glad to see the back of. In either case, try to make it clear to your reader why you feel that way (even if it's not very clear to you when you start to write, the spur of having to put something down on paper very often clarifies your thoughts during the writing process).

(b) *A Letter to* ...: an old friend or relative, alive or dead; fan-mail to a star, alive or dead; or a "Dear John" letter breaking off relationships (which don't have to be romantic – you could be explaining to a pet why you're having it put down; telling an item of clothing that's passed its sell-by date why it's being thrown out; saying goodbye to a favourite old garden tree/rose bush/gnome – any sort of breaking-off). The main point of the exercise here is that you're addressing the person or thing *direct* and not explaining your feelings to the world at large. So bear this in mind when choosing your explanation as to why you're writing to them: are you releasing venom because someone's hurt you? Indulging in some hero/heroine worship on the page? Or apologising for the inevitable march of time resulting in something wearing out? Decide the tone of your letter before you begin and choose your words accordingly. Or you can use your letter to apologise for what you never said/did while they were alive or in contact with you, explain your motives – or simply have a good rant and tell them off!

(c) *Desert Island Thoughts*: rather than limit yourself to 10 Desert Island discs, like the famous BBC radio programme, to take with you to listen to when you're marooned on that desert island, this exercise allows you a whole range of activities. You might well start with 10 pieces of music, and explain your choice in writing. But this is an on-going exercise, something that you can keep adding to by allowing yourself 10 of any of the following:

food:	starters/main courses/desserts – or limit yourself to 10 *items* of your favourite food;
clothing:	your 10 favourite items of clothing, and why you'd want them with you (this will probably mean forgetting the 'Desert' bit);

people:	assume 10 others are marooned with you: who would you want/be able to put up with/find most useful?
leisure pursuits:	to while away the time, you can have 10 items, e.g. a football; pack of cards; Monopoly game; book of crosswords; television.

You can probably add more areas for yourself as your list grows (e.g. 10 books you've always wanted to read or wouldn't mind re-reading). In many ways this is similar to Assignment 3 at the end of this chapter about compiling a Joy-List: a celebration in writing of what you enjoy most.

Exercises

(a) *Visual Stimuli*: re-read any writing you were able to do in response to Section 3 in this chapter. What was your overall reaction to the idea of visual stimuli? How do you think you may be able to expand on this and use it in the future? In your Learning Diary, record which bits you found most useful – or even if you didn't find this section useful, can you say why? Using the notes you've made to do with Visual Stimuli, can you think of any object, painting, photo or drawing which will never fail to represent each idea and thus remind you of one writing source? The connection will be purely personal – it may simply be a picture of a pen or could be a Giles cartoon … even that Oriental lady!

(b) *The Creative Process*: understanding the methods used to go about writing is as important as the finished product – once technique is in place, it can be re-applied to different ideas.

Answer the following questions for yourself:

- Which aspect of the writing process comes easiest to you, and which hardest? E.g. finding the right words? Thinking up metaphors, similes, etc.? Describing someone close? Dredging up old memories?
- How easy/difficult do you find it to self-disclose on the page?

- Are you able to conjure up images easily and absorb the mood of a place, or are you a very 'concrete' thinker, who observes well and records data first, mood and atmosphere second?

Your responses to the above questions will tell you what sort of writing you'd be advised to stick to: if you're a concrete thinker, try non-fiction; if you're an imagist, try fiction or poetry. If personal disclosure is too difficult, use fictional characters to speak through, rather than autobiography.

Assignment 3: Joy-list

Whenever you experience something that makes you feel good, jot it down. Then when you're feeling thoroughly miserable, re-read what you've written- perhaps you could elaborate on an item if you find you've already recorded it once. You could either include this along with your diary entries, or make a separate entry.

As one of my own poems begins:

> *"My glass is half-full.*
> *Why is yours half-empty?"*

See the end of this book for the full version of this poem.

4 Using your life story

SECTION 1: STYLE
Historian or storyteller?

YOU NEED TO DECIDE AT THE VERY start just *how* you're going to use your life-story in writing yourself well. It won't serve any useful purpose to dredge up old memories just for the sake of it – but will this perhaps help you to finally look something in the face, analyse it, and put it emotionally 'on file', rather than have it sitting in the in-tray? Catharsis in psychological terms means 'the purging of the effects of a pent-up emotion and repressed thoughts, by bringing them to the surface of consciousness'. Writing can be cathartic as it articulates ideas and thoughts that we may feel unable to talk about elsewhere. If that is our purpose in examining past events, objects or people in our lives, then the 'historian' approach to autobiography will be inappropriate. (The 'historian' approach means showing how your experiences reflect the life and times in which you've lived.)

The 'story-teller' approach, however, should prove far more useful. Simply writing out your autobiography as one long confession, or a long list of facts, will neither endear you to any prospective readers (should there be any), nor help you understand your feelings and motives in the cathartic sense. But turning a major element in your life – the one aspect that's caused you the most pain/nuisance/struggle – into a tale exploring human relationships, reactions, addictions, etc., and getting that 'down on paper' will hopefully help in that purging process.

So a first decision to be made in using your life story is – who's doing the talking? Autobiography usually uses the 'I' form, and you may find it simpler to talk through your own mouth initially. On the other hand, making that first big step into writing anything so personal may leave you feeling in need of some protection, some anonymity – and creating a fictional character to do your talking may be the answer. Try looking at yourself and the events you're describing as if through the eyes of someone close to you – the all-seeing Fly-on-the-Wall, or verité, approach. This will also allow you to include everyone else's feelings and reactions. But it will mean talking about yourself in the third person – 'I' becomes 'he' or 'she', – and this makes it less chatty, more a tale being told than a good gossip over the garden fence. What the third person does do, however, is make your story attractive to any reader rather than just to those who know you, rather more of a novel than an autobiography.

A medium well-suited to the story-teller notion is the short story: this can vary in length from a 'short short' of about 250 words through to upward of 7000 words. Try writing up a variety of incidents as if they were mini-tales – don't worry too much about the formalities of structure or beginnings, middles and endings at this stage – but think in terms of the possibility of these being a collection eventually, or even made into a cohesive whole to form an autobiographical novel. 'Memoirs' as a literary genre are a written record of personal reminiscences, but don't *have* to be told in the first person – and you can even produce a Diary format missing out altogether either an 'I' or a 'he/she' and just using diary jottings (e.g. "10.00 am: caught the bus to town; met Jed in the café" where we don't know who's catching the bus, etc.)

American author Mary Karr had always been interested in the memoir as a genre; however, her own childhood memories were so painful, and she'd suppressed them so deeply, that it took 30 years of therapy and talking to those nearest to her before she was able to write it all down. It was a deeply moving process, but despite this the result, her memoir *The Liar's Club*, concentrates on the most difficult and painful years – and is told through the eyes of a child. It still manages to be very funny at times, despite the horrors that she suffered – and therefore perfectly readable. For the telling of traumas like this, using the persona of a child means that adult judgements and considerations acquired with the hindsight of later life can be missed out completely. You only have to state facts and how you felt about it at the time – no remorse, thirst for vengeance, need to apologise. Let your reader be the judge.

Polemics

A 'polemic' is a controversial piece of writing or argument, written firmly from one viewpoint. It can be a tirade against someone or something if you're not careful and you allow yourself to get carried away once the pen gets moving. We have just talked about not letting remorse or bitterness take over your writing: you can use the written form of expression to let some of this go, but try to be constructive about how you look at it and learn from it, rather than have a nasty spillage of something caustic all over the page.

The same goes for your ideas and beliefs as it does for emotions. You may be driven to write because you hold strong beliefs that the rest of the world doesn't seem to be taking on board: you have a point to make and will be viewing everything with this in mind. Get used to toning down the hard-core polemics in a way that will make your ideas more presentable to other people and not have you sounding as if you're riding your hobby-horse without ever dismounting from it! To do this, you can use anecdotes from your own experience as proof of what you believe; or simply be as factual as possible without passing judgement. The exercise in Chapter 3 "Letter to the Times" – can be used here, for you to practise.

Humour

If you've an incident from your own experience to relate, but you don't want to name names, you can always use a parable or allegory. This is one incident taken as an example of a wider truth: one person's particular experience shown as being typical of what could happen to any of us. Often the main characters are referred to as e.g. 'the boy', 'the old man', 'the fat woman', rather than giving them individual names, because they are representative. There may be a moral to the tale, or you may use it for purely entertainment reasons – but either way, humorous treatment will lighten not only your writing but hopefully your spirits as you record it.

Even if the incident you're recording isn't intrinsically funny, turning it into a parable may help. Other ploys: insert any humorous dialogue you overhear or can remember; or after the ending, ask yourself 'What if …?' something hadn't ended that way, but had come into play to alter the run of events. You may end up with a piece of writing *based on* an autobiographical incident, which you've then used to demonstrate a point in a humorous manner.

In order to criticise modern-day life, writers also very often use *the absurd or grotesque*, exaggerating what's likely to happen or what did actually happen out of all proportion. Again, if you don't feel able for whatever reason to 'tell it like it was', have a think if you could possibly use exaggeration in this way, or even cartoon-style anecdotal recording in words, with humorous results (if you can draw, even better).

An incident is longer than an *anecdote*, and covers a whole minor episode so will have something resembling a beginning, middle and ending. An anecdote, on the other hand, looks something like this: "Once Gran had moved in with us, there was no getting rid of her. She was an all-seeing, all-knowing presence, the embodiment of conscience. You even felt guilty breathing too loudly. But she had her uses, as they discovered next door when some kinky burglar who'd failed to break into the house made off with the contents of the washing-line. The Police Constable who came to our door asked me for any small clue I might be able to give, and Gran's voice piped up from behind me: 'There were four G-strings, all black, and two pairs of men's Y-fronts. Can't remember the rest.' The PC and I looked at each other, and burst out laughing."

Note the speech marks: frequently in an anecdote someone is being quoted direct; there may even be a punch line similar to the final line of a joke. The style of an anecdote is one of a brief description of a situation, straight-faced, and then it's what someone *says* that provides the humour. In your writing, you may find it convenient to collect both incidents and anecdotes by theme, i.e. on a related topic, – the sort of themes that recur in everyone's life story writing, such as sexual exploits; money (or lack of it); trouble at school/work/with the police; learning to cook/drive/change a nappy/change a tyre/change a plug/etc.

Exercise: Turning an anecdote or incident into a short story

For the above anecdote about Gran and the underwear, the basic facts for a short story are there: perhaps the would-be burglar was an addict, so how did he get that way? What happens next – the story may continue with the underwear being found and an arrest. Was it someone the writer knows? You have to decide where you'd begin and where end, then fill out the middle (NB – do it in this order). Ask yourself:

- Is there a possible twist for the tail?
- First person narrative, or third (I or he/she)?

- Does it demonstrate the mood of the times (is it a social comment)?
- Is there a moral to the story/could it become a parable?
- Should I introduce any other characters, and if so, which?
- Will the story suffice as it is, or should I fill in "what happens next"?

After you've had a try at turning the above into a short story, can you think of any suitable anecdotes or incidents from your own background that you could use in the same way?

SECTION 2: CONTENT
Putting yourself in context

Heredity and Environment: the two major areas that make up human character. Are you aware just how these two areas have combined to produce the way you think and behave? Inherited characteristics are something we may not be aware of until later in life – and if you haven't known both your parents you may never be in a position to assess their influence. On the other hand, already as a youngster you may have found someone telling you: "You don't half take after your mum/dad" – and probably when you were only seven or eight you may have thought that this was nonsense!

The environment we grew up in cannot be underestimated as a strong influence on us all. Are you a product of the inner city, a suburbanite, or from the countryside? Ever bothered to think what difference this may have made in your life? Try it: try putting yourself into a different context and asking "what if ...?" A whole range of factors go to make up that 'context' or environment, and whether you felt totally at home in it and part of a family, community and society, or felt ostracised and on the edge of it in some way, you can't escape its influence.

Besides the more obvious elements such as class, ethnic background, religion, education and sexual preference, there are economic circumstances (often wrongly confused with class – a self-made man with money can retain his working-class attitudes, or the income of someone with middle-class attitudes may be minimal); family circumstances; physical or mental impairment. All of these will have contributed in the formation of you as a person, and recognising this puts you in a position to excuse yourself if you feel guilty about any one element from your background. Until we are adults, we can't be expected to break free from what heredity and our environment have lumbered us with – or to appreciate the good influences and say 'thank you'. However, once our inherited characteristics and the environment we grew up in have done their bit, we have outside events and our own personal choices coming into play to shape the sort of person we are: living through a world war, for instance, and whom we choose for a life-long partner.

Exercise: "There's something in my genes!"

Thinking of how family tendencies have affected you, make two lists – "For" and "Against". Even before you were born there will have been every chance that you would turn out to be good with your hands/ athletic/overweight/a genius/a natural-born talker ... or the opposite of these. The list is endless. So what is your inheritance? If you're not in a position to judge – perhaps you never knew your parents – you can still make a similar list looking at yourself as you are now, and realising which are the inherent characteristics.

Using your list, decide which bits you'd like to improve on or do away with altogether, which bits you're happy with, and which parts of you you've given up on as a hopeless case. Do a write-up explaining why you think that way, as if to someone who's never met you. Include any feed-back you've ever received from other people – you may well hate one aspect of what you've inherited, while many other people appreciate it, or at least aren't troubled by it the way you are.

Creating a life graph

In order to look at our life story as a whole, it's useful to be aware of the high points and low points. Try applying the notion of a graph to your life: what stands out as being a particularly bad or good time? You may want to jot down notes first in word form, as memories occur, then in order to draw a graph re-arrange these into a linear time-scale. Is there a slump revealed that you weren't aware of, or perhaps your life-graph is one long straight line with almost no high points and low points? If the latter is the case, have a re-think: what criteria are you using to judge 'high' or 'low' points? Happiness is perhaps the first criterion that springs to mind when we think of highs and lows – but what about achievements?

Exercise

Try working out 2 separate simple graphs, one for happiness and one for achievements, then impose one on top of the other to see where they cross. There is every reason to believe that the highs, the lows *and* the points where such graph lines cross will be the most revealing about ourselves, when it comes to deciding which incidents and events to use as a basis for writing. Does your life-graph look as you'd expect? What *key themes* does it reveal – e.g. are the high points, as you see them on your graph, times when personal relationships have been going particularly well? Or when you've been winning things/making money/progressing your career/enjoying a holiday/have moved house? How important has the material world been in your high points?

You may now decide that if you're to use your life story from which to start some form of writing, you only want to examine one of those key themes to begin with: concentrate on the happiness high points and what caused them, for instance? Or do you want to plunge straight in to look at the whole thing, warts and all? For a lot of people, the latter choice may be off-putting – so start with what you know will give you pleasure to talk about on the page. You may find as you get used to more regular writing that you're able to cover some of those low points that at first seemed too painful.

Rose-tinted spectacles, (or looking back on old times and forgetting the painful associations)?

One of the most difficult things about writing autobiography is telling it like it was: you may not even *remember* it like it was! In order to avoid painful memories, our memory bank will often either obliterate details altogether, or colour them a delicate shade to make them look more presentable. A little tentative enquiry round the subject, talking

41

to others who were there at the time, may put things into a different perspective – someone else closely involved may remember the same events very differently from the way you remember them.

The opposite is also true. What appeared horrific to you as a child, for instance, and has been stored in your memory in that light, if it happened in adult life would seem relatively insignificant. Be strict with yourself: are you exaggerating memories for better or worse, and if so can you put them more into normal perspective? This doesn't mean to say that when writing about feelings and events from the past you won't need to record the rose-tinted or horrific version that has stayed with you. But what you will need to do is make it clear to your reader what is the 'truthful and accurate version' that the rest of the world observed (and perhaps reported on), as compared with your personal reaction. In trying to give your readers this insight, hopefully you'll gain personal insight into why you reacted the way you did.

Hearsay, gossip and nostalgia

There is also a danger of edges getting blurred with time, concerning what actually happened and what was hearsay. If we want to believe something sufficiently, our minds find ways of turning something told to us into gospel events, without bothering to check the facts. Be careful! You may end up being sued for defamation of character, slander, or something similar, should your writing become public. If you need to check local or national events from the past, use the facilities which the library service has to offer to do so.

But a lot of hearsay takes the form of gossip, the malicious version or just someone having a thoroughly good natter. As it gets passed on from person to person within a community, or from generation to generation within a family, details can get altered slightly – so that what you are eventually told may have started out with quite a different slant to it. Add to that the time element of passing years – and perhaps a dose of nostalgia thrown in – and a picture may emerge that's rather a long way from the facts.

Nostalgia, according to the dictionary, is "the desire to return to some earlier time in one's life, or a fond remembrance of that time, usually tinged with sadness at its having passed". If our lives have been particularly traumatic, it may be difficult to pick out such a time – you may have to narrow it down to just one particular holiday that proved very enjoyable as a child, for instance, or a short spell living in a particular place. But this is an excellent starting-point for using one's life-story in writing: from the narrow focus of one short spell that you regard with nostalgia, you can branch out, as suggested in the following exercise:

Exercise

Briefly describe one incident or one place from your past (either distant past or more recent past) that you regard with nostalgia, using about one side of A4 paper. Try to do this spontaneously as you remember it. Then ask yourself the following questions regarding the incident or place, and make notes of your answers:

1. *Why* did this particular one spring to mind? Was it one happy island in a sea of misery? Or the best of a fairly boring bunch?
2. Was it the *people, the place, the events* that made the difference? Or any other one element that you can think of?
3. Do you suspect yourself of wearing *rose-tinted spectacles* regarding this? Or have you other factual back-up, e.g. other people's memories of this time?
4. Do you think this was in any way fundamental to determining your *future attitude* to either people, things or places like this?
5. Whether your answer to (4) is yes or no, follow this up by making notes explaining why you think that way, given the hindsight of time.

Symbols

A symbol is an image or object endowed with meaning. From our past, a particular object will serve to remind us of a happy time or place, or an unhappy one – it will have come to represent something. This will be true only for ourselves – no one else is going to look at that same item and be affected in the same way. A tatty old rag-doll will look like a tatty old rag-doll to everyone except its sole careful owner – for whom this is a trusted friend called Topsy with a background and context. You and Topsy have 'done time' together: she may be a fellow-sufferer or someone who's shared all your childhood secrets. The same could apply to anything from an old cricket bat to a photo to a clock you inherited, which sat on the mantelpiece and observed family conundrums for years. We may not still possess the object and may have forgotten about it – only when we spot something that reminds us of it will the memory-association be sparked. It may not even be an object – a family pet may look like an ugly old dog to everyone else, and it's difficult to appreciate why anyone should be in mourning over its death. But in the same way as a family heirloom acquires significance because of its history – who has used it, sat on it, worn it, over the centuries – a pet will have become a family member or a long-standing partner if you're alone, with associated memories of walks in favourite places, and so on.

In order to describe an object effectively, you will first need to consider the factual, technical side of its appearance and function, before superimposing on that anecdotes about how it was used, who said what about it, how it featured in your life, etc. A third 'layer' on top of that will be the emotional significance related to it. Assume you're describing it to someone who's no idea what it looks like. Describe the overall outward appearance without taking any of it apart – first impressions – then *where* it used to stand/where it lived; *who* used it; and *how* it related to you and those around you. What we don't want is a process analysis of how it worked or step-by-step instructions.

Then ask yourself if there is/was any one particular part of it that has always fascinated you, and try to explain why. The family desk that I inherited has a secret side compartment with four little drawers hidden behind: as a child, being allowed to look inside these was the ultimate adventure. They mostly held boring old family papers – passports, copies of my parents' wills, etc. – but the simple act of opening something up to 'see what's inside' cannot be underestimated for a seven year old. That desk now stands proudly in our dining-room, 50 years older and more battered, but has stored archives of memories for me (to anyone else it's just a battered old desk!)

Your initial description will be objective rather than emotional, but from there you can then add humorous or nostalgic overtones to give spice to the bald facts ... that 'meaning' referred to in the first sentence of this section. Make it clear what it was, what it looked like, the part it played in your life – then relate the fond memories.

Exercises

(a) *Describe a Favourite Toy or Game*, either played by you as a child, or which you've played since, remembering to give some indication of how it was played, where and when, as well as who with.

(b) *Describe either a pet's, or a beloved object's appearance*, and explore in writing why it means so much to you. What would the rest of us see, looking at it?

(c) *"A Favourite Meal"*: does any one favourite meal from the past spring to mind? Do you know what was in it? Did you make it, your mother, or was it when you visited a relative or a restaurant? It doesn't have to be a whole meal – just one item of food will do – but your description should cover the technical side if possible (how it was cooked/what the box or tin looked like, its wording and any instructions) and any special occasions on which it was eaten.

Assignment 4: Your inheritance

Is there anything you've had handed down to you that you definitely could have done without? This could be anything from red hair to flat feet, a grandfather clock to a piece of jewellery. Or is there anything that *failed* to be handed down that you would have really liked (the ability to play a musical instrument or prowess in sport, for instance) as well as any object you were particularly fond of? Is there anything of yours that you're looking forward to handing on – and will the next generation want it anyway? This is a list that can be added to over time, but start now to explain in writing what you see as your inheritance.

5 Attitudes

IF YOU'VE NEVER HAD OCCASION TO write about your attitudes, beliefs and values before, it may well prove as hard as if you were being asked to write a love poem for the first time. Deeply held convictions may have remained undisclosed to the world for years, with neither time nor reason for you to consider why you still think that way, whether you really do believe that credo – or why on earth you should go to the lengths of writing about it. If, however, events have taken a turn causing you to question previous attitudes or to waver in your beliefs at all, writing down your thoughts can help enormously to clarify them. So where to start?

1. *Ask yourself what formed those attitudes.* Parental or other family influence, perhaps? Were you born into a particular religious or political creed? Remind yourself in writing – e.g. by describing how those beliefs manifested themselves. What can you remember about how you felt when you first became aware of this aspect of your mental inheritance – proud? Disgusted? Curious?

2. *How have those attitudes changed* over time, if at all? Are you now at the opposite end of the political spectrum from where you started out, for instance? What happened, either to instigate change, or to entrench you in those convictions?

3. *Discussing your attitudes*: has this been difficult in the past? Or was it simply irrelevant, something you weren't interested in doing?

4. Was there *any one person* who influenced the way you think, or was it more a matter of the environment and class background you grew up in?

5. *Optimist or pessimist?* – which are you? Can you say what there was in your background that made you tend one way rather than the other?

6. *Motivation*: have you a driving force, a 'mission in life' to get on with, that motivates you to continue in the direction you're going? Or has that motivation run out? Perhaps you're simply

bowling along life's highway with no aims or convictions to steer you? Is anyone around you like that – and can you assess what's delightful about that attitude, and what's annoying?

Exercises

(a) *Individuality*: do you feel other people have imposed their standards on you, or are your life-rules self-imposed? Are you happy to be 'one of the crowd' and follow others' lead – or would you rather do your own thing? What do you think has made you that way? Can you think of any examples from the past to demonstrate this? If so, describe what happened, how you felt then, and how you feel about it now, looking back.

(b) Describe in about 200 words one person who was influential in shaping your attitudes;

(c) Describe any one element in your background that had a similar lasting effect.

Fears and concerns

In 1995, the Sunday Times printed an article about the differences between children's fears and concerns 20 years previously, compared with their worries in 1995. Interviews with more than 1,000 children aged 7–12 revealed that global and national considerations such as war, killing animals, bombs and guns, crime and homelessness, had entered the top 10 fears and concerns. It was suggested that this may be because of national and world events being seen on television, and the effect of conflicts being shown on TV news, making the whole scene appear nearer to home and therefore worrying.

What were still included amongst major worries, however, were the 'old favourites' such as spiders and creepy crawlies, the dark, bullying and cruelty – the sort of childhood concerns which tend to repeat themselves generation after generation. And something like fear of spiders can stay with you for life – perhaps one small incident in your childhood may have dictated how you will view spiders, or any other insect or 'creepy crawly', even though in later life you know it's not rational.

Exercise

Make a list of your top 10 fears and concerns, as a child (if you can remember!) and now. How have these changed? Using your 2 lists, build sentences either making statements or asking questions, then put these together to form a continuous piece of prose. Are you able to say *why* fears have remained the same, or a new set has formed? Imagine you're explaining to someone who doesn't know your background.

One way of coping with fears – childhood or adult – is the 'hands-on' approach, showing the worrier in detail what the feared *object or animal* looks like and how it works, thinks or behaves. In writing terms, try a factual description of the object or animal: breaking it down into its component parts makes anything more 'real' and removes that aura of the unknown, and hence the fear, with which we may have imbued it. Or we can give character to something: a lot of children's literature features weird animals or objects that turn out to have human characteristics and even speak fluent English, rather than coming over as horrific monsters. Dragons become forgetful, old and fumbling, or friendly but suffering from a bad breath problem, for instance, rather than breathing fire.

Exercises

(a) Take some *everyday object* and think of a situation where it could reproduce itself to take over the world, e.g. pollen, and write a short story describing how it does so;

(b) *Genetic Modifications*: either an animal species or a plant has been subject to genetic modification in a laboratory – with unexpected results! A new, hardier sub-species is formed, and human beings have enormous problems controlling its reproduction and the subsequent continued survival of other life on earth. Work out your details, and then write a TV or radio news bulletin special, announcing a warning to the country about what's happening. Choose your language carefully, so as not to panic the human population.

(c) *Machines* or electronic devices: something that's supposed to be inanimate appears to have designs on taking over the world – or at least its immediate surroundings. This could be a computer running amok, JCBs (diggers) forming an army on their own with no drivers, or mobile telephones communicating with each other in a conspiracy. Alternatively, the machine or device may be the innocent instrument being used by ghosts or aliens: your satellite dish is receiving messages that it's not supposed to, by accident. Where from? What do these messages convey? Devise a code form that they come in; then describe the scene when you first discover what's happening.

Coping with *situational fears* requires a little more ingenuity. These tend to fall into two categories – the unknown (e.g. the dark, falling off a cliff, ghosts) or coping with actual people (e.g. bullying, abduction, physical abuse). Either of these categories may manifest itself in a nightmare or bad dream, where the dreamer feels helpless in the face of danger; fighting back proves to be a useless exercise; fleeing is interminable – you just go on and on being pursued down an endless flight path, or falling, falling, falling. Modern-day science fiction, horror and crime novels use these themes continually: they are now standard situations for writers' characters to find themselves in, whether it be up a dark alley, back to the wall as human threat closes in, or exploring a new planet and encountering hostile monsters.

Can you think of any situations in your everyday world where those same feelings of helplessness or being pursued might be caused? Someone being stuck in a relationship they feel unable to get out of, for instance, may invoke similar feelings, or bullying at school? If you do suffer in this way or have done in the past, you may well make a good writer of horror or science fiction stories: try turning your experiences into fiction. You may not want to use the 'I' form – that may be a bit too near to home – so first you'll need to create a character as the centre-point of your stories, a hero or heroine who can boldly go anywhere and survive. Or perhaps a monster, dragon or machine that may look horrific but in fact turns out to be able to solve all sorts of problems that we mere mortals can't.

Exercises: "Alien landscapes"

(a) You have been dumped in an alien landscape, either in wilderness on earth or a foreign planet, and left stranded. Nothing looks

familiar. Design a set of instructions for yourself, under the
heading "Don't Panic", a step-by-step guide that can be used by
others who might follow you in such a situation. This will include
how to cope with any human, alien or animal beings you may
encounter (and the ensuing communication problems).

(b) Describe your *feelings* on finding yourself in this alien landscape.

(c) *"An Ideal/Nightmare Landscape"*: have you a photograph, an old
calendar picture, or a painting depicting your idea of an ideal
landscape? Or have you a vivid picture stored in your imagination
of where you'd ideally love to live, spend holidays, or just wander?
It may not be a palm-fringed beach of pure white sand under a
permanently blue sky, – it could be a windswept Hebridean
moor, for example – but try to describe it by picture-painting in
words. To give the flavour of the place, use metaphors, similes and
onomatopoeia (see Chapter 3(d) to remind you of what these are).

And then the opposite! What would your nightmare landscape look
like? The sort of place where one has to struggle to survive, full of
threats and dangers? The term 'landscape' tends to make us think of
countryside rather than the city, but a nightmare landscape could in
fact be a townscape, the centre of a city full of skyscrapers and back
alleys, railway sidings and dead docklands.

In writing either of the above, you may find it helps to draw your-
self a map, to include all those best and worst features that spring to
mind as you start to think about landscapes.

Loneliness

The novelist Rose Tremayn had an idyllic wealthy childhood com-
plete with nanny, in Chelsea – a part of London with a reputation
for all that money can buy. But when she was only 10, her father left
home, her mother had to move house, and Rose was sent off to board-
ing school: in one fell swoop she lost everything familiar to her in the
way of physical and emotional environment. She started writing to
combat the loneliness. Once upon a time, children would have poured
out their woes or frustrations to a teddy bear or similar toy; told a 'best
friend'; or if telling someone aloud wasn't an option, tried drawing or
writing. In today's world, a child in a similar situation might well have
a computer to talk to – even key into the Internet – rather than pick

up a pen, but if you're already an adult it's a perfectly natural reaction to let a page know how you feel. Diaries and journals can replace the human confidant(e) in such circumstances.

And today's society can still come up with plenty of situations where loneliness can take hold, despite the ease of electronic communications. You may find yourself growing old without a partner – due to divorce, bereavement, or never having married, or feel trapped in a destructive relationship. The 'empty nest' syndrome is a recognised phenomenon suffered by many women (and men for that matter) once children have grown up and fled the nest. With or without a career, you may find yourself asking "Where to next?" having discovered a big hole has just appeared in your life. A hospital bed may be surrounded by the bustle of a busy ward, but if you're unable to leave it and verbal communication is difficult the result is much the same as it is for the housebound – isolation. And for carers – those committed to looking after the disabled or terminally ill – joining a social group of any sort may not be viable, so the effect is the same as if you were housebound.

Adult Creative Writing classes always have a notable intake of men in their 50's and 60's, many of them newly-retired, or having been made redundant. If you've spent many years working in an office or factory surrounded by people with whom you've communicated verbally, even if not intimately, it comes as a shock to the system to find yourself with very few, or even no, people to talk to. Finding yourself without a job at any stage of life is often a lonely experience, especially if financial circumstances alter and you're no longer in a position to keep the same company you once kept. Depression can often set in, a frequent partner to loneliness.

Or you may have moved house – moved country even – and find yourself in a new area without friends and any sort of familiar environment. You may be in the position of having friends or family elsewhere to write to, and this often provides a lifeline. How we approach isolation of whatever type will depend on attitudes towards self-sufficiency or dependence on others: quite simply, can you cope on your own? What we mustn't do is try to apportion blame: loneliness is so often the result of a particular set of circumstances, and not someone's *fault*. There is frequently a tendency for someone suffering loneliness to believe that somehow they've 'done something wrong' to deserve it, that they can't get on with people or are anti-social, or to blame a body that seems to be packing up on life and cutting off its owner from the rest of the world. Even if we don't try to blame ourselves in some way, for someone made redundant, for instance, there is always a government or employer to blame; for the divorcee, acrimony and alimony often go hand-in-hand.

Exercise: Analysis

Have you ever been lonely? Or do you know someone you would class as lonely? Before something can be cured, we need to know just what caused it and how it manifests itself. It's not enough just to say "I lost my job" – many people do so, but manage not to suffer loneliness as a result. Ask yourself the following questions, and jot down your answers (applied either to you or someone you know):

- What were the *events* that caused loneliness? (e.g. job loss, bereavement)
- What have been the *mental effects*? (depression? numbness?)
- Any *physical effects*? (e.g. a stroke; weight gain)
- Have these circumstances caused *loss of confidence*?
- Has *fear* been a feature? What fears have you/they experienced?
- Has *sense of humour* been affected?
- Has *social interaction* been affected? (e.g. bothering about appearance; nervousness; mannerisms)

Now ask yourself what you think would solve each of these by being firstly realistic, then allowing your imagination to run riot. For example, 'finding a new partner' may be a practical possibility to solve being on one's own … then imagine what an *ideal* new partner would look like, sound like and behave like.

Next, using the above check-list as a basis, write an appraisal of either your own or someone else's situation, diagnosing what has caused loneliness, how the person concerned has coped with it, and what answers, if any, there are for loneliness in today's society.

Truth and lies

The term *poetic licence* means 'an allowable departure from strict fact, rule or logic for the sake of effect, as frequently occurs in poetry'

(Chambers Dictionary). Whether you're going to attempt poetry or prose, however, you can use poetic licence for a variety of reasons – e.g. to protect yourself from recriminations, should anyone you've talked about decide to take legal action against you, or to protect others from what might prove hurtful to them.

This may take the form of transplanting someone's character into the body of an animal or object: Selima Hill in her poetry changed her mother-in-law into a 'rabbit or giraffe' in order to give herself the freedom to let go of the reins and be emotional through a disguised voice. Use the 'innocent' voice of a child to talk through, to get a different perspective on the truth, the truth as a child sees it being different from the truth as an adult may see it. Or undergo a sex change when you start to write, and try looking at the opposite gender's idea of truth. You can also enter a time-warp – move events back a century or two and write as if your story were historical fact, or forward into science fiction; or change place, and set your story in the Mediterranean or South America (if you're sufficiently familiar with another part of the world). This is the sort of licence taken when you see a TV film or drama classed as 'fact-based' – you don't have to tell the truth, the whole truth and nothing but the truth. If we did so in writing the whole time, the result would read like a court report. The basic underlying emotion or pain will still be yours, the point you want to make won't alter, but the who, how, when and where may be changed. The 'what' is that poetic truth.

The last hundred years have seen the erosion of *taboo subjects* which, certainly during Victorian times, weren't talked about: death, grief, child abuse, sex, for instance. But just because we can now see documentaries examining such subjects in detail whenever we turn on the TV doesn't mean that we personally find it any easier to discuss them openly. We may gloss over such topics, not just in conversation with others, but also to ourselves. Taken to extremes, this can result in outright denial – "It didn't happen". The newly-widowed old lady will still behave as if her spouse is around, leaving his slippers in their usual spot or talking about him as if he's 'just popped out'. To cope with bereavement we continue to address the departed, either mentally or out loud.

When it comes to writing as therapy, however, we have to be honest and open with ourselves first: acknowledge what was previously taboo to one's own psyche, and then see about how writing could be used to help us cope with it.

Exercise: "Being discovered"

One half of a couple has a secret. The couple in question could be a middle-aged married couple, two newly-weds, people of the same sex who live together, friends who see each other regularly – but whoever your couple are, you will need to reconcile the type of secret with their age and background. For instance, has one person sworn to give up drug-taking but is secretly still doing so? Or is one partner being unfaithful, unknown to the other? You will probably find it easiest to decide the secret first, then create characters to whom this secret might apply. Make notes for yourself first about the couple concerned, their ages and backgrounds, jobs or lack of them, how they came together in the first place, etc.

Now describe the confrontation when the secret is discovered, with one person challenging the other. The 'guilty' party tries to bluff it out at first, denying everything and in his/her defence accusing the other person of being paranoid and making it all up. Include:

– Background narrative about where and when this takes place;
– The conversation/shouting match in dialogue;
– Body language: *how* both parties look throughout;
– The outcome: does violence erupt, one person storm out threatening recriminations, or are tears and apologies the result?

Ever been conned? A couple of years ago, the BBC TV police/public crime-solving programme *Crimewatch UK* had a case featured where a con-man went round visiting little old ladies who lived alone, pretending to be a policeman and clearing off with their money. "He seemed perfectly nice" was one comment. Deception for financial gain in this way has been practised for centuries – by both men and women. Such cases make splendid material for the crime fiction writer: "What sort of person could deceive innocent members of the public like that?" we ask in disgust, on reading the details in the newspaper. And when we see the perpetrator on TV, or their picture in the papers, they look 'perfectly normal', like any other man or woman in the street. What bothers us, the general public, is that although they can pass themselves off as one of 'us', their values and thinking are far removed from what is considered generally acceptable. The morals and scruples that prevent the rest of society from this sort of deception for personal financial gain seem to be totally missing in such people.

A Venus's Fly Trap is "a type of insect-eating plant with hinged leaves that snap shut on insects that land on them". The human version of a Venus's Fly Trap could be either a real-life type out to deceive and make a quick buck, a con-woman who attracts men like flies and relieves them of their cash, or you could have the sci-fi version, some sort of monster that lures. A human Venus will need to be perfectly feasible – she (or he) will look 'nice' and 'normal' as we've already discovered is how con-persons appear in their chosen cover role. Film roles along these lines in the past have included the male bigamist who marries lonely wealthy widows to obtain their money; in today's terms, we could perhaps include a prostitute or 'female on the make' who compromises a politician on purpose, and then either resorts to blackmail or sells her story to the press.

Exercise

Design a 'Venus', then write one episode as if for television where he/she successfully 'lures' someone into a trap – but can you do it from Venus's point of view, explaining the thoughts going through his/her head at the time? (i.e. worrying about whether cover has been blown and always having to look over a shoulder). If you don't want to write any actual dialogue, map out in note form the plot structure, the basic storyline, which your episode would cover.

Bystanders

Are you one of life's bystanders, who will always stand by and watch it happen? Or will you try and prevent it if you think it's wrong, or make something happen that you think ought to be happening? Ever been guilty of that shrug of indifference, that 'It's nothing to do with me – why should I intervene' attitude? And afterwards, have you regretted your inaction, or regretted having taken the side of the majority because it was safer, the easy way out, rather than standing up for what you thought right? Self-preservation often leads us to stand by and watch, and keeping one's head down can become a way of thinking in all areas of life, if we let it. Consider the following scenarios:

1. Two men and a woman are in a car, which draws up at traffic lights. The woman gets out and starts to run away. One of the men follows her and starts beating her up. An elderly man passing by starts to go to her aid when the man still in the car shouts "Be careful – he's got a knife". The elderly man walks away.
2. You are in the middle of a busy shopping arcade when a middle-aged woman a few yards away sinks to the floor with a groan and slumps down against a shop front. Everyone else takes no notice and carries on with their business.
3. A woman in your railway carriage is being verbally abused by two drunken men. It reaches the stage where they threaten rape and violence, and pour beer over her. Only when they get off the train does anyone move to help.
4. At work, you're about to enter the toilets when you hear a row going on inside. One of your colleagues bursts out, leaving another colleague sobbing and/or injured inside.
5. A pub disco is in full swing when a waitress who's collecting glasses comes across a body unconscious on the floor. She goes to inspect it and is jumped on by two women who attack her until she passes out. The crowd stand and watch.

If you were there, what would you have done? And would it have been any use, do you think – would any action you took only have resulted in two injured bodies instead of one, or two embarrassed people? Should people act as a matter of principle in such cases, or turn away? Why do you think the people described in nos. 1–5 behaved as they did?

Exercise

Have you ever witnessed something and been a bystander, rather than taking action – and have you regretted it since? If so, use your own experience and describe your feelings at the time and how other people reacted (in the case of no. 3 above, an actual incident, one policeman who arrived on the scene became very angry with the bystanders, whom he described as being 'struck dumb, deaf and blind').

Or take one of the scenarios described above and look at it from two points of view: that of the sufferer, and one bystander. In the case of the latter, relate their thoughts at the time as if they're making a *confession* to the page and trying to justify their reasons for not acting; or perhaps they are feeling guilty when they discover that the victim concerned died, remained permanently injured, or in the case of no.4, lost their job through no fault of their own?

From the sufferer's viewpoint, try writing their press or TV *interview* given afterwards. This will involve thinking up the questions your interviewer might ask and writing them out together with the victim's answers – but as in any such interview, the personal, emotional aspect will be probed by the questioner.

Conformity

In the previous section we were looking at inaction – being a member of the crowd because it was safer and far less hassle to do nothing – the negative side of things. Conformity may result from positive choice (a decision to be an upstanding member of society because you want to be) or from pressure to conform. Whether you're aware of it or not, there is pressure to conform being pelted at you everywhere you look via advertising or newspaper headlines cajoling those who don't conform. Conforming means moving with the times and adopting what's fashionable (and automatically liking it) – or being classed as at best a bit of a 'fuddy-duddy', at worst an outcast. Or it can take the form of being told what you're supposed to dress and think like – or else! Large corporations have dress-codes for their employees, for instance, imposed because of the image they wish to present to the world, and which they think the world wants to see. This will involve appearance generally, e.g. hair (both facial and hair-style) as well as the type of clothing worn.

The state, the church, our schools and institutions have their ideas about how we citizens should look, think and behave, so that even if there's nothing remotely criminal or deceptive involved – even if someone is simply standing up and saying "I don't want to do this" – if you don't toe the line they expect, they think there's something wrong that needs putting right.

One manifestation of this attitude that we're particularly fond of in the United Kingdom is *uniforms*. Have you ever had to wear a uniform of any sort, either for school, your job, or for a leisure activity? How did you feel about it? Were you perfectly happy to do so, proud to be identified as one of a distinct crowd – or was it a straitjacket for you? Were you longing to burst out of it and 'do your own thing' clothing-wise? If it has never occurred to you to rebel, even as a teenager – why not? It's almost expected (almost a matter of conformity?) that at such an age we start to throw out tentative feelers in the world, to start to adopt a life-style that may be far removed – or only a little removed – from that of our parents.

On the other hand, perhaps you're a born conformist. There is, after all, supposed to be safety in numbers ... or are you completely in tune with the thinking of the majority anyway? Never felt the slightest desire to chain yourself to any railings as a protest? Can you think of any one cause for which you would be prepared to 'stand up and be counted' – to sign a petition, lobby your MP, take part in a protest march, etc.?

Exercise: "Tree house"

'Chips' Malone is the last remaining protester in the tree house built in one large oak tree at the edge of Sandall's Wood, which is due to be cut down to make way for a motorway extension. Inspector Gerrard from the local police force is making a final attempt to talk him down, armed with a loud hailer and backed by several uniformed officers and a police dog. Set the scene in a brief prose narrative, then write the dialogue between them: Chips is maintaining he represents a last stance against officialdom's sledge-hammer; Inspector Gerrard is 'only doing his job' on behalf of society in general, whose representatives have sanctioned the motorway (i.e. it's been approved officially).

Assignment 5: "Outlook on life"

1. "I'm the sort of person who expects the same from other people that I'm prepared to give, and is frequently let down."
2. "I never make demands on other people – why do they always make such demands on me?"
3. "I am the sort of person who can organise other people's lives, but not my own."

59

4. "One of these days, I'll show the world how clever and talented I really am!"
5. "I am the sort of person who always falls in love with the wrong partner."
6. "I always worry about other people's opinions – I don't want to look stupid."
7. "I always wish I'd done it or said it differently after the event."
8. "I seem to be stuck with these bad habits, so I might as well accept I'm like that."

Above is a selection of statements, any one of which – or several – may apply to you. You may well be able to add to the list as you begin to think about your outlook on life. Decide just how you would word your Outlook Statement as it applies to you, then elaborate on this in writing, to explain to the world what makes you tick. This is an on-going piece of writing that you can add to as and when ideas occur.

6 Alone or in a group?

MOST PEOPLE WHO TURN UP AT creative writing workshops or courses have already 'had a go' on their own. Adults have usually worked out roughly what they want to say, decided what type of writing they'd prefer to try (invariably the type they most enjoy reading), and then ... aren't sure where to start. The first few tentative efforts may have proved unsatisfactory, and we often show those efforts to our nearest and dearest, who are the worst possible people to give clear, impersonal feedback, as they're so closely involved. So we realise that we need outside help if we're to progress.

In the case of writing, in order to feel better, there may be no need to 'progress' visibly with one's writing – simply continuing to enter thoughts in a journal or diary, for instance, may be enough to get something out of the emotional system. Or to lay one's worries out on the page – to 'see what you're thinking' – may help to assuage them. Or you may already be in a one-to-one tutorial situation with a therapist for your writing. And for many, the idea of going public to the extent of reading what you've written to a group, or letting them read your thoughts on paper, may be very off-putting. If you're happy writing on your own, you're finding it useful – and you have books like this one to help! – you may not feel the need to move to a writing group.

However, should you decide you've reached an impasse with your writing – perhaps writer's block has set in – or you want to make a start, and you've noticed there's a group in your area advertising itself that looks interesting: what advantages are to be gained from joining a writers' group, and what sort of set-up will you find if you do so?

Advantages of joining a writing group

(a) One of the main advantages frequently expressed by those coming to a writing group for the first time is that they're *not the only one* with a similar set of problems. As with all types of groups you may join – sports clubs, social clubs, professional societies, leisure activity groups – just discovering that you're among people who feel the same and react the same, have the same problems and interests, is already therapeutic. A problem shared is a problem solved!

(b) Within a group, you can choose to be as *anonymous or conspicuous* as you wish. You only need divulge to anyone else as much or as little as you feel able. At first this may prove very difficult, but as you become more at home with one group of people, an 'opening up' often happens. Or you may wish to remain under the shield of anonymity throughout.

(c) Writing at home on your own, it's far easier to get things out of proportion. Even in a one-to-one tutorial situation (e.g. with a therapist), your thinking may remain self-centred, and your problems may seem enormous and all-consuming. Finding others who have similar – or worse – problems, and discovering how they're coping, very often *puts things back in perspective.*

(d) *A widening of viewpoint* can be achieved in a group. Others may have faced exactly the same problems as you, but reacted very differently (and successfully) in a way that hadn't occurred to you. The more people who contribute to a group's 'life', the greater the breadth of information that can be shared, far more quickly than if each individual had to suss out all that data for him/herself.

(e) *Feedback* on how others see you and your writing may not be what you feel up to receiving at first. Any criticism of your writing may feel like a blow on the chin to start with – so you may want to remain anonymous until you feel you're among friends. Then feedback can be very helpful – these are, after all, people who are there for the same reasons as you. Feedback does need to be constructive: criticism for the sake of pulling someone apart will help nobody.

(f) *The discipline of writing to order* when a group meets and tries out an exercise, or in a workshop situation, may be what is needed to marshal the brain and turn on the inspiration (which if left to itself can be very slothful). In order to write, what you may need is a jolly good prod – and a writers' group can provide this (but see (d) under Disadvantages).

(g) For those of us who don't talk easily and aren't used to self-disclosing out loud, one advantage of a writers' group is that you can come along with *your contribution written down*, or at the very least write your ideas down during the group meeting. The result can then be read out, if you feel unable to join in a discussion spontaneously (cf. the next section in this chapter on the set-ups different groups have).

Disadvantages of joining a writing group

(a) *Group management* plays an important part in ensuring all members feel at home and are not side-lined by one or more predominant characters imposing themselves and their ideas on the rest. One bossy loud-mouth, or a resolute non-conformist, can change the whole ambience of a group from being friendly and welcoming to having a fraught, quarrelsome atmosphere.

(b) Where a writers' group is made up of very like-minded individuals, there is always a danger of *too much similar thinking*. So the breadth of opinions mentioned in (d) under Advantages doesn't come about.

(c) Members may feel afraid of *hurting someone feelings* when giving feedback – so you don't gain an accurate picture of your writing, but are led to believe whatever you write is brilliant. We may not like criticism, but at least it makes us think about what we've produced and the way other people may react to it.

(d) *Writing to order* is something most of us, when starting out, find very difficult. A writing group will come together for perhaps 2 hours a week with the intention of actually producing some writing on the spot during that time. Even for experienced group members the mood may not take them, inspiration may not strike – it may simply be the wrong topic on the wrong day. (In this case, the answer is to have the best of both worlds – take the ideas gained in the group home with you, chew them over, and then explore them in your writing when inspiration does strike.)

(e) For those whose *literacy level* is low, a writing group may not be the answer. Finding others who are happily churning out perfect sentences on a page when one's own effort is produced only with a massive struggle may only serve to increase a literacy inferiority complex. At home on one's own, grammar, spelling and a regular flow of words don't matter.

(f) *Dogma and prejudice* can rear their ugly heads in any writing group. One individual, or a small pressure group within the main group, may have distinct ideas of what's acceptable writing and what isn't. The debate about whether poetry should rhyme, for instance, continues to crop up whenever a new writing group or class comes into being. Again, whoever is running the group will need to ensure that minds are kept open and creativity is allowed its leash, or a stilted, one-sided attitude to creative writing can result.

This flows over into areas connected with all the other types of prejudice we may encounter: is the group going to be open to everything from rap poetry to the latest soap opera to hit our screens? Or will some subjects be taboo?

Writing workshops

Creative writing is usually taught in what's described as a 'workshop'. Other creative subjects such as painting, photography, sculpture, handicrafts, often have sessions described as workshops also. The term is borrowed from the old manufacturing workshop idea, where individual workers are either making one item on their own, each at their workbench producing a separate finished product, or each is completing their own particular phase of a process to which all in the workshop contribute. In either case, a supervisor will be going round ensuring that each worker is making progress, and helping them with their problems.

Applying this to creative writing, each person may have their own particular piece of writing they want to get on with – there may be a novel at the back of someone's mind as the ultimate goal, or the intention of turning on-going diary-keeping into an autobiography. The 'supervisor' in this case is either a tutor, or group organiser co-ordinating efforts. Group meetings therefore have to allow enough breadth of topic for each member to be able to take *something* from it, and apply it to their long-term project. This may be done on the spot, or a session's content can be taken home and applied to the long-term project there. Each session may well be on a different writing skill, or a different genre, but there is no way every session can cover the interests of all of the people, all of the time.

Many beginners, however, don't have anything long-term in mind, and are there to experiment, to find out what type of writing suits them best, so workshops based on the skills of writing in a variety of genres are often a good idea to start with (See *Starting to Write* from Studymates). In the case of writing for healing purposes, this last scenario will probably be the case. More important initially will be the mutual support a group can give to help get some sort of writing started, and the sharing of experiences. What will no doubt emerge as a group 'gels' are a set of common themes to be explored further in writing (see Suggested Topics List at end of this chapter). Everyone can bring their different problems along to work on (the equivalent of an individual, on-going project), while topics can be chosen for discussion and writing at each session that reflect overall themes related to human nature.

Features of writing workshops

1. Despite the suggested Topics List later in this chapter, one main element about workshops is that they should be totally *flexible* and able to be adapted to suit the needs of the individuals attending. So even though a pre-arranged topic is usually a good idea for a workshop session, within that topic elements should be easily adaptable. An organiser will need to keep his/her ear to the ground as to what suits people best, and always offer *options* – choice for written exercises, how long to spend on one area as opposed to another, etc. As writing is generated in response to ideas put forth, there should be opportunity for a group to 'follow its nose' and go off in a direction not previously planned, if this appears to be working well, rather than have a route already dictated.

2. *Balance* must be maintained between being too informal and too formal. Beginner writers need more structure to a workshop session than do the more experienced – the idea of 'being left to get on with it' on their own may not be something they've come across in school or even in the workplace, so a good deal of guidance is needed to start with. This probably means that when someone is struggling to write on their own, within the workshop setting, the supervisor, tutor or organiser will have to spend time with that person to encourage them to get started 'doing their own thing'. Balance also

means allowing everyone their say during discussions, no matter what that say may contain – but also allowing equal time to all.

3. *Sharing* is another major feature of workshops – not only sharing opinions and ideas but even sharing one's writing when one feels able to do so. This doesn't necessarily mean having to share 'in public' by reading out loud to the rest of the group, but could be limited to letting a group tutor have a look at what you've written. Sharing may even take the form of a joint group exercise or project where everyone is part of the team to a greater or lesser extent. Or your contribution to the group can simply be in the form of talking *about* the problems and advantages discovered during doing a particular piece of writing on your own.

4. *Feedback* for therapeutic purposes needs to leave out the criticism, but use what someone's read out to stimulate discussion and the sharing of ideas. Remember to talk about form as well as content. If you want good feedback from what you're reading out, ask questions before you start: explain how you came to write the piece and what your qualms are about, for instance, whether you've chosen the right format, whether it's too long or too short, whether it's not really finished off properly, etc. Then your listeners can watch out for these elements as you read your work out loud, or they each read the written version.

5. *Tutor/leader participation*: a writing workshop isn't a class, and this isn't school! As well as examination of other well-known writers' work being a major element in a workshop, tutors or leaders should be prepared to read out their own writing, or hand out examples of it – and have this used to spark discussion in the same way as anything else examined. But when chairing discussions, a group leader has to remain impartial and not let personal preferences and prejudices run the show.

6. *Practical Arrangements*: the following elements have been found by other writing groups to be essential for success:

   • *Atmosphere* needs to be friendly and make sure all feel welcome; new members should be able to feel they'll be taken seriously no matter what they write; that those present care about their progress; that they become part of a team who will encourage them no matter what;

- *Time and Place* need to suit members: too short a session, and participants will feel pressured into trying to write something too quickly, resulting in frustration; too long a session, and concentration will fade. Spending too much time on one area will bore some people: with a flexible schedule, you can order things so that everyone has a 'taster' of a topic or style of writing, and then those who want to spend more time exploring it can have time allotted during the following session, while others do something else.

  And as with your individual writing, you need to feel comfortable in the particular place chosen for a group to meet. Many writers have their favourite desk or armchair where they frequently produce their best writing; similarly, a group's writing environment needs to be conducive to inspiration. Don't expect your poetry to flow when there's a JCB (digger) loudly smashing concrete outside the window! One example of this that I experienced was when a local authority group I was taking, which had been meeting in a rather cold community centre, didn't have sufficient numbers to continue – but could all fit round my dining-room table. The more formal tone that had been prevalent in the more formal setting quickly gave way to a warmer, chattier atmosphere – and the writing began to flow accordingly.

  For those working in the areas of mental health and with the disabled, the time of day was also important: when is the group at its most receptive? A quiet spot at a quiet time of day will prove invaluable.
- *Seating Arrangements* for any discussions taking place need to be face to face, rather than in a classroom-style, all-facing-teacher format. Desks for writing on can be arranged e.g. in a horseshoe or three sides of a rectangle (where a blackboard or visual inspiration, for example, is involved on the fourth side). This enables everyone to see everyone else, and all to be heard more clearly when reading work out.
- *Facilitation/Co-ordination*: I have been talking about 'tutors' or 'group leaders' as being in charge of writing workshops – but a group leader may in fact be a chairperson newly-elected each year. The job for all leaders will be basically the same, though: to suggest topics for sessions; design exercises if required; chair

discussions; allot time-chunks to each element of the session; keep momentum going.

- *Contributions* in the form of newspaper or magazine cuttings, leaflets, advertisements, book details, or the mention of TV/radio programmes: group members should be encouraged to bring in to each session whatever they've spotted, to share with others.

- *Sub-grouping and Pair-work* may prove a practical option if a group is large enough. A group of about six people is sufficiently intimate for sharing and self-disclosure to take place, but for larger numbers splitting up into smaller elements will enable people to get to know each other and each other's writing at a more personal level. Imagine having to read out your first written effort to a group of about 15 people you hardly know – far better to have the opportunity to share it first with one other person or a mini-group of about four or five. They can then either make suggestions for improvements, or encourage you to go ahead – with their 'backing' and support – and share what you've written with the whole group.

  So with larger groups, it's a good idea to choose a workshop topic that can be split into smaller sections, with either pairs or sub-groups each given one area to deal with (see suggestions list at the end of this chapter). Afterwards, the results (either findings as a result of discussion, or writing produced) can be shared with the whole group. Such a final session is known as a plenary session. The advantage of doing it this way for a larger group is that a far wider area can be covered during one workshop: time would not allow for each individual to cover each element. It also means that *all* concerned have reason to feel they've achieved something, even if an individual's contribution has been small. There is also opportunity for those better-skilled in one area to help those less skilled – but the organiser will have to ensure that someone isn't 'trampled on' by their pair-work partner or the rest of the sub-group so that they take nothing from the session.

- *Group Tasks*: as mentioned previously in the description of what the term 'workshop' originally meant, a workshop can have each member doing something separate but contributing towards a whole project. This allows people to pick out which aspect of a topic they'd most prefer to write about, rather than having to cover the whole thing. Being part of a team working together, you have a sense of needing to 'get on with it' in order not to let the rest down. So *some* writing gets produced some of the time. This could take the form of each member developing a character they've chosen from a set of characters already designed in outline; or two members of the group writing a piece of dialogue – one scene for radio or TV, for instance, – while others develop the storyline and characters. Those working in the area of mental health, however, have found that when using writing as therapy, joint group tasks of any kind don't work too well as those taking part progress at such different paces. It's preferable to develop individual writing programmes tailored to the specific needs of each participant.

1. *A Typical Workshop Session*: having attended a variety of writing workshop set-ups (everything from disabled writers to those without an official leader, who take it in turns to organise sessions), I have found certain core elements are common to all – but there is a much wider range of options that can be chosen depending on a group's preferences. Most groups, for instance, find members clamouring for some sort of 'homework', a writing task to take home to ensure that they feel obliged to get some writing done before the next session. A two-hour session's timetable may contain some or all of the following:

- *Feedback from the 'homework' task*: either reading out of writing produced, or discussion about problems encountered. The reading may well be done by the group leader – even those experienced at reading out their own work often want to hear what it sounds like when someone else reads it out;
- *News session*: the sharing of writing-associated information; members' own progress: who's written what since the last meeting;
- *Subject for the session*: a topic session, or a genre session? It's a good idea to choose one or the other and not fall between two stools – but it will depend on members' preferences. Do they want information and details about how to write in a particular genre (e.g. Japanese verse-forms; TV sit-coms)? Or are they

happy with form, but want to look at possibilities for expressing their ideas in a variety of forms (e.g. lyricism in prose and poetry; depicting landscapes in writing)? A co-ordinated series of sessions often works well – once interest is aroused, people want more of the same. So when choosing session topics, ask yourselves "What spin-offs could there be from this?"

- *Hand-outs*: extracts from literature, magazines, the local press, etc. or any other writing for people to read for themselves first is always a good idea. After seeing how others have gone about either the topic or the genre, you can then have a try on your own at something similar. If it can't be photocopied, perhaps it can be stuck up on a board for each to read, or at the very least a short extract can be read aloud and main points noted ready for … .

- *Discussion*: either following on from material read, or resulting from the group leader introducing the topic briefly. How does everyone feel about writing like this? How did you react to the piece you've just read? Any ideas occur immediately to set you writing? And so on.

- *Writing session*: most groups will try to do *some* writing 'on the spot' during a session. This may only be preparing a list of some sort, e.g. 'points to include' if you were to write about the topic under discussion – or just jotting down rough ideas;

- *Plenary session*: the 'coming together' after individual writing, to compare notes and see how everyone got on. Those who want it can now ask for feedback on what they've produced. Very often 'homework' will be finishing off what's been started during the workshop.

Options above and beyond the basic session contents just listed could be any one of:

- *Theory session*: a taught session explaining the theory behind a particular style of writing or writing movement. This could be conducted by the tutor or group leader, or could be by a … .

- *Guest speaker*: one attraction of attending a writing group is that you may well have the chance to listen to an experienced writer talking about how they came to write, or various teachers of creative writing widening your viewpoint on what options are available. Or the speaker could be a professional from another walk of life who has used writing in their work, e.g. psycho-therapy; criminal investigations;

- *Field trips* apply to writing groups in the same way as they do for botanists or geologists! A walk along a country lane, or a beach, in summer can be used for making notes to write up later: the impressions gained from looking and listening, the odd meta-phor or simile that occurs while you're actually there, can be jotted down. Or a trip to the theatre, a museum, stately home, gardens, or a national heritage site can be used in the same way, the aim being to produce a write-up afterwards. The write-up can come in the form of anything from a journalistic report for a local newspaper to a poem.

- *Sub-grouping and pair-work*, as mentioned under no. 6 (above) can either be used during an indoor session if the topic lends itself – or a field trip can start out with this in mind, with two, three or four people covering one area to write up. This narrows things down so that if time is short, more details can be covered. For instance, a visit to a stately home and its gardens can be split into 'architecture', 'the rose garden', 'the glass houses', 'those who lived here', etc.

- *Psychodrama* is an action therapy in which a group member acts out real or imaginary scenes from his/her life, with other group members playing the parts of significant people in their life. This allows the expression, amongst a sympathetic 'public' (i.e. the group), of anger, hurt or frustration: an airing of something that may have remained suppressed for a long time, in order not to hurt other people, open up old wounds, etc. Applied to creative writing, each individual writes a short script – a piece of dialogue, or one scene for a play, radio or TV, for instance – with characters created using those close to them as models. Names can be changed, ages and places altered, but the emotions being expressed will be very real. The result can either be read out completely by the writer at the group session, or if copies have been obtained, various members can play the 'parts' as in a play-reading.

Role-play on the page can also be done in pairs, with a little more help in the form of each pair in the group being given two characters already designed in outline, plus a situation in which they find themselves. The pair then have to compose the ensuing dialogue – which could be, for instance, a row, one chatting the other up, or question and answer. The two characters may even be in the form of a drawing, photograph, advertising poster or cartoon handed over to the pair – but it's up to them to make the characters 'real' and imbue them with human feelings that come out in their dialogue.

- *Case studies* are a useful item to include one per session. A detailed scenario is put before the group, either fictitious or taken from real life experience, and discussion follows as if in a consulting room. The questions which the group leader might put are something like: What would *you* have done in this situation? How do you think this situation came about in the first place – what went wrong? How do you feel about the characters portrayed here? The group is then asked to continue the storyline with "What do you think happened next?", or to write down the advice they would give to one or more of the characters. Notes are then compared during the final plenary session.

- *On-going project*: if the group has any one project to which all are contributing in some way, each session will need to leave a small amount of time for this. Perhaps the group is putting together an anthology to publish locally; another group project that I've experienced is the joint writing of a pantomime, with characters devised by different people, scenes written and then one group member co-ordinating the whole.

- *Brainstorming* is a feature not only of workshops but of management sessions in industry and commerce. The group is asked to say whatever first comes into their heads when a subject is mentioned – and carry on doing so for a few minutes. It's the written version of 'first impressions', before you've had time to mull over what the topic means to you in more detail. The group leader writes down these single-word or short phrase instant contributions, and discussion follows from there. Often our immediate reactions give away our prejudices, likes and dislikes and true opinions, whereas given more time our inhibitions come to the fore and we think before we speak. The idea of brainstorming is the instant generation of ideas by getting people to speak first, think later.

This method can always be used to get things moving when a new group has been formed or a completely new subject area is being broached. In creative writing terms, asking for single adjectives, for instance, to do with a topic results in a list that can be used for everyone to try and include as many as possible in a poem; or a set of names/jobs/children's cartoon characters can be brainstormed and then used as the basis for a short story.

If a group does have inhibitions about brainstorming out loud, however, or the size of the group isn't conducive to it, the same process can be done via each person writing immediate ideas down on paper during a short time-limit, then the group leader can go round asking out loud for contributions. This also ensures that one or two of the more forthcoming members don't hog the limelight.

- *Visual and aural stimulation*: objects such as paintings, photographs, ornaments, or music of different kinds, can be used as the basis of one group session, or a series of sessions. Group members can be asked to bring in examples and the results looked at/listened to, then members' reactions described in writing. To avoid anyone being upset, however, by disparaging comments about taste, it often works best if one or two objects or musical items are chosen by the group leader for use in any one session, and the resulting discussion guided towards e.g. memories sparked by the object, or what one can visualise on hearing the music.

Exercise: Visualisation

'Visualisation' is a therapeutic technique used to alleviate disease in many cultures. Rather than having an actual object in front of you (on your own or in a group), the idea is to choose something pleasant, perhaps a favourite ornament or an old toy that's dear to you, in order to evoke feelings of peace and happiness. This also covers experiencing e.g. a pleasant walk in the country; entering a kitchen as a child, where your favourite food is being cooked; and as just mentioned, what you visualise on hearing certain music. All five senses are called into play (sight, sound, smell, touch and taste). It may well help to cut off one of your senses in order to magnify the others – i.e. to close your eyes for a short spell while visualising. Having chosen an object or experience, jot down those sense impressions that come to mind immediately while still fresh, plus any happy memories that have been evoked, or incidents associated with it, and pleasant feelings.

Vivid visualisation, with practice, should lead to feelings of well-being and happiness, and ultimately should help to alleviate pain (see Tulku Thondup: *The Healing Power of the Mind*).

Who is suitable for group therapy?

As already mentioned under (e) in Disadvantages of Joining a Writers' Group, those whose literacy level is low probably won't benefit from a writing group – but that won't exclude them from other forms of group therapy. We also discovered in Chapter 1 under 'Precedents' that in the area of mental health, individual one-to-one therapy proved far more useful than group work. Anyone severely depressed or withdrawn will not be up to joining a group – you need to be ready to interact with others for mutual benefit. So that also excludes those who are perfectly ready to 'interact' as *they* see it: the hypochondriac who only discusses his/her symptoms all the time and doesn't contribute constructively to group life, or the narcissist who cannot see beyond his/her own enormous ego.

People with low self-esteem are also unsuitable for group therapy, as they don't tend to be able to disclose their deepest thoughts and feelings, and when they do so, the 'truth' is often embroidered for effect and the impression they can make on others. Honesty and openness is a pre-requisite in a group therapy situation: if someone is lying to themselves about their condition – and to other people – they aren't ready for group therapy.

The support a group can give will benefit anyone feeling socially isolated and struggling to cope on their own (even if surrounded by other people offering support – it's still possible to feel 'they don't understand as they haven't experienced what I'm going through'). Those who see authority of any sort as an automatic problem, if they can build up a relationship with the tutor/group leader, may well manage to fit into a group, perhaps while remaining on the sidelines, but taking something away with them they can use. In their case, a one-to-one writing therapy situation may well smack of a teacher/pupil scenario.

In the case of the Chronically Sick and Disabled – either bed-ridden, a wheelchair user or similar – a group situation can be a major support, if it can be arranged. Creative writing in recent years has gone into hospitals very successfully; one group I have had close contact with in the North-west of England meet intermittently to write, and produce their magazine three or four times per year. As usual, the main inhibitor for them and any other disabled groups around the country trying to find a venue is wheelchair access, suitable toilets, etc. Creative writing hardly needs other special equipment, unlike a sport – writing can be done in a small space, it makes no noise nuisance and doesn't cost the earth to buy a pad and a pen … . So in theory there could be a disabled writers' group in every community centre that has access. One added advantage of a disabled writer actually managing to be present at group meetings is that this may give them access to a *scribe* to do the writing for them, if they are able to dictate. Carers at home may not have the opportunity or inclination to fulfil this added role on top of everything else, and of course inspiration may only strike once given the stimulus that a writing group session can produce.

Exercise: "How do you feel about the idea of a writing group?"

Ask yourself the following questions, then put your answers together into a coherent statement summing up how you feel about the idea of joining a writing group.

1. Having read the section entitled "Who is suitable for group therapy?", do you think you would be? What leads you to this conclusion?
2. Do you normally look forward to meeting a new set of people, or is this usually something which worries you?
3. Would you be worried about spending so much time and effort integrating with the group that any writing you might do would suffer?

4. Would a major concern be the standard that others in the group might already have achieved, leaving you far behind?

5. Conversely, would you be worried that others in a group situation might not be as committed to serious writing as you?

6. Would you prefer an all-male or all-female group, or a mixed one?

7. Would you be put off by the idea of self-disclosing to others during group discussions?

8. Would you be bothered by someone else plagiarising your ideas for writing purposes? And how would you feel about borrowing theirs?

9. Are you already a member of any other form of group? Describe it, and any significant role you have played in its development (e.g. secretary). Are you happy with this group's set-up?

One development in recent years that is making the idea of belonging to a group open to consideration by those isolated at home is the Internet. For writers this is but a small step from tapping away on one's own computer alone – and you can give yourself an instant readership for what you've written! It does, however, only offer response and camaraderie for the writing side of things. Many writers' groups, once established, appreciate the 'being there' physically, having to get out and meet people who have become friends regularly: the socio-emotional element in belonging to a group. The Internet can do a lot for those physically isolated, but can't show you the light in someone's eyes.

One-to-one writing therapy

When you are in a group, there is less obligation to produce some writing as others can contribute and keep the group going. With a one-to-one writing tutor or assistant of some sort, there's no escape! You are 'on the spot' to respond to questions asked and tasks suggested. On the other hand, the whole arrangement is tailored to your individual needs, so you should be able to do a little dictating, at least, regarding what writing you achieve. And your tutor will not be in the position of trying to suit as many people as possible, as often as possible, when designing session content. So you have someone all to yourself to answer questions and offer guidance.

As already pointed out in the previous section regarding who is suitable for group therapy, one-to-one writing therapy covers more specialist areas (e.g. mental health) or may be used prior to someone joining a group to raise confidence and start the writing habit. In my own case, I began writing as a result of one-to-one writing therapy, having had an emergency caesarean due to eclampsia, followed by a coma and total memory loss. Recording every detail in writing as the memory was slowly restored was one major method used for recovery. But facts were fuzzy: emotions were far more real, and it was significant that my first creative writing was in the form of poetry (see Chapter seven on Poetry for Healing).

It is possible to have the best of both worlds – one-to-one tutoring within a workshop group. But this will depend on time and how many are in the group: can one tutor get round everybody individually, or are there several helpers to do so, as may happen in a disabled group? An audience of one isn't going to give you an enormous breadth of response to what you've written, but on the other hand a complete beginner may be more prepared to take criticism from someone whose expertise they know and trust, a sort of writing confidant(e).

Group writing therapy topic suggestions

Elsewhere in this book is a whole range of ideas that can be used in a group situation, but the following suggestions are split into 'topic' and 'genre' sessions. Also included here are ideas for possible division into sub-groups or pairs.

Topic Sessions	*Sub-groups/Pair-work*
1. Childhood and how it influences later life	Sub-groups to each compile list of elements relevant, e.g. family
2. "A Day in the Life of Me" – and how I feel about it	
3. "Why me?" – positive and negative aspects of character	
4. "I'm stuck with these genes" – inherited characteristics	

5. Is the family dead? (and would that be a good thing?)	Sub-groups to compile 'for' and 'against' lists
6. "In another life, I'd like to come back as …" – and explain why	
7. Desert Island Thoughts: would you survive on a desert island? If so, why? If not, why not?	Pair-work: interviews similar to the radio programme of the same name
8. Portrait of an Angry Young Man/Woman: designing a 'character' that typifies how you think of an angry young person. How would he/she talk, dress, behave?	Sub-groups to do a 'photofit' in words
9. Dreamscape: describing (a) your worst nightmare (b) your idea of bliss	
10. "The pen is mightier than the sword": true or false?	Sub-groups for debate
11. "Am I boring you?" – audience awareness; what to tell and what to leave out, and why	Pair-work: testing a piece already written on one other person
12. My favourite room/My ideal room – a description of what makes you 'at home' in a place	
13. Accusations, insults, slander and opinions	Sub-groups: what annoys you most, resulting in a Top Ten list per group

Genre Sessions — *Sub-groups/Pair-work*

1. "Lonely as a cloud": metaphor and simile – what they are and how to use them/be original	
2. The Good, the Bad and the Ugly – film and TV heroes and heroines: who likes whom, and why	Sub-groups compile list of qualities
3. Body language: reading others' minds by their actions	

4. Renga: Japanese group poetry	
5. A letter to … an old friend or relative, alive or dead	Pair-work correspondence
The Times newspaper	(Its editor replies)
'Dear John': accusing or parting	('John' puts his point of view!)
6. My favourite quote – and explain why	
7. Group's own MORI poll re. this century's best poem/film/novel	Sub-groups then consensus
8. Top Ten novelists/writers/poets/ journalists	Sub-groups then consensus

The ideal number for a writing therapy session is not more than about 8 people, which should allow everyone to have their say who wants to, but not make those who are more reticent feel as if they've been thrust into a spotlight. More than that number, and sub-grouping or pair-work may be needed. No one should feel forced to join in, or to accept feedback/criticism. It should also be made clear from the start that anything divulged during a session won't "go beyond these walls".

The writing process is as important for therapy as the finished product: knowing *why* you've written something and being clear as to the best order to put something across so that people understand you. These aspects need to be considered throughout, so group members will be encouraged to read widely and ask questions like "Why has he/she written it in that order?" Extracts of writing handed out during a session can be examined in detail to see how others have expressed their feelings and ideas, and then used as models to produce something similar. When group members have shared their writing, they can also share their inspirational process to answer questions like "What made you come up with that idea?"

One danger for a writing group of any kind is that everyone may become so friendly that gossip takes over and hardly any writing gets done. The group leader will have to remind the group that the purpose of them being there is to manage some writing – even if this is only a few notes to take away and expand on. Another danger for the individual is being a minority of one, and being afraid to say so. If you disagree with the consensus of the group, it doesn't mean to say you're wrong – you're perfectly entitled to your opinion. But the rest may want to know *why* you think that way, so you'd have to be prepared to explain, which may put some people off attending a group.

Assignment 6: Individual writing programme

Design your own Individual Writing Programme: set yourself targets for pieces of writing you'd like to get done, and give yourself a rough timetable in which to achieve these. You may want to include some or all of the exercises and assignments in this book – or use these in conjunction with an on-going writing project. If your aim is to write your autobiography, for instance, try to organise yourself so that you write so much per day/per week. Many professional writers such as novelists go about their writing like this, often writing at a certain time of day and aiming to have the next chapter finished by such-and-such a date. This will get you into the *writing habit*, in the same way as a regular group session of any sort would necessitate having a go at *some* writing, even if only something very short.

7 Poetry for healing

IN CHAPTER ONE, I STATED THAT "for many writers-in-residence dealing with people with short concentration spans, poetry was found to be more useful than prose". I then went on to cover the lighter verse-forms such as rhyming couplets that can be built up week after week to form a longer poem. The exercises that followed at the end of Chapter One (The Fruit Game/Furniture Game/Use of Objects) were intended for either prose or poetry – as are many of the exercises throughout this book.

Several factors may put people off having a try at poetry. For a lot of people, their only contact with poetry will be reading classic poets such as Keats and Wordsworth in school, and the more mainstream twentieth century poets. The resulting dissection of poems to learn about verse-forms and the tools used to create poetry produces a whole new language to be learnt, the language of prosody. The myth is propagated that in order to 'know about' poetry you'll need to speak this language and have specialised knowledge in the same way as to use a computer you will need at least *some* 'computerspeak'. And that's just to understand other people's poetry, never mind having a go at writing it yourself!

In fact, if you can write reasonably coherent English – or produce a line out loud for a scribe to write down for you there's no earthly reason why you can't attempt poetry. Poetry can remain like a set of jottings in a way that prose can't: by its very nature it is shorter and you don't need complete grammatical sentences (but you still need some punctuation to indicate where the pauses occur, question-marks, etc.) What should be stressed to the complete beginner, having a go at writing poetry for the first time, is that you don't have to be initiated into an exclusive 'poetry-speak'. Some of the most beautiful poetry is in simple format. If you want to pursue your interest and find out all about iambic pentameters, for instance, then my own Practical Poetry Series, books 1–8, (Cherrybite Publications, 1998, ISBN 1900447 28 2) covers most aspects of the technical side of poetry writing.

Poetry's uses in healing

Poetry is a very useful medium for the expression of *emotions*. Frequently the bereaved turn to poetry for comfort when it may have played little or no part in their previous everyday life. Why? Because they can appreciate that the grieving poet whose words they are reading has gone through just the same sort of emotional upheaval as they, the reader, are now doing. They are not alone. Others have been there before them, and survived: survived loss by the death of, or desertion by, a loved one.

Poetry has also been used to excellent effect in Special Education for a number of years, in assessment centres and special schools. Even the most anti-authoritarian or illiterate youngsters manage to write some sort of poetry, and in doing so they express very painful or deeply hidden emotions that they are unable to talk about. And in the case of dementia sufferers, nursery rhymes which rely heavily on repetition and imitative sounds- are a natural outlet. So it is but a short step to try something original in the poetry line bringing together all these elements for people who do so naturally (especially where stringing together longer sentences to form prose may not be an option).

Considerations before attempting to write poetry

The technicalities of poetry-writing can be learned if you have the inclination – but are not necessary at the outset. It's far better to gain enthusiasm by having a good look at poetry generally, seeing what's been written in the past and what's acceptable as poetry, and then choosing what you'd like to try.

There is such a wide choice of poetry-writing open to the beginner that, in the same way as I always ask would-be prose writers what they enjoy reading most, and suggest they therefore have a try at that particular genre first (crime fiction, love stories, sci-fi, etc.), I make the same suggestion regarding poetry. That may mean introducing someone to several whole new concepts in poetry writing to see what they like the look of and indeed what they like the sound of.

So before you can choose what poetry form to try, you need to know what's available. Many people will never have seen a prose poem, for instance, or read any of the short Japanese verse-forms (haiku, tanka). Or you may have spotted some poetry and think you'd like to try and write like that – but don't know where to begin or what's involved in that particular format to make it poetry. Some serious thought and discussion regarding 'what makes it poetry?' while looking at both good and bad examples might be a good place to start – but not *too* much dissection. There is always a danger that over-analysis will destroy the magic of a finished poem, and the purpose here is not criticism but to get some idea of what makes the poem 'tick', in order to attempt something similar oneself.

Exercise: Re-writes

Find a well-known poem that you admire, the sort of poetry you wish you could write, and try re-writing it either on a different topic or from a different viewpoint. To do so you will need to 'borrow' the original's rhyme-scheme (if it has one) and any discernible beat, metre and repetition. If none of these is immediately apparent, read it aloud: where do you find yourself pausing (always at the end of a line – or is there running-over from one line to the next?) Does slant-rhyme become audible, that subtle half-rhyme which a glance at the page may not indicate at all? Have a look at the original's syntax – which words are placed where – and see if you can replace them with your own words of similar length/number of syllables. Alternatively, try writing out the original omitting its nouns and verbs – then insert your own.

Another major consideration if you're approaching poetry for healing purposes for the first time is whether to make a particular *genre* your own and specialise in that type of poetry, or have you a *topic* you wish to cover which can adapt to any poetry style? You may well not be sure until you've looked at what other poetry-writers have tried in the past – or until you've simply had a go yourself and seen the result. It may narrow itself down quite naturally to one particular genre – the sonnet, for instance – or you may find examples you like in a wide variety of poetry and can't choose (you don't have to – try a variety!)

What has happened over time is that certain genres have come to be associated with certain topics: the sonnet for love poetry, for instance; the elegy for grieving; the limerick for humorous poetry. You will only be able to decide what works, in your opinion, by reading widely. You may reject all the more formal verse-forms and want to try blank verse (which has some sort of rhythm and metre, but doesn't rhyme) or free verse (which does its own thing completely!); or perhaps syllabics – counting syllables rather than the number of beats per line.

And how do you feel about rhyme? There is still a body of opinion that wants poetry always to rhyme – but you may well find when you do get that pen moving that you can write flowing free verse with no trace of rhyme. If you have qualms, try deliberately writing some lines that don't rhyme, and then introduce rhyme at the end: what is the effect? Sometimes this may result in a 'jangly' effect which isn't wanted – or does it help the *sound* of the lines? As always with any poetry you write, try reading it aloud (and seek a second opinion if unsure).

Should you find either that you prefer one poetry genre to others, or that you have an overriding theme you want to pursue over a wide variety of genres, consider the possibility that your first few tentative attempts at poetry can be built up towards something bigger. Don't set out to produce just one poem, end of story. Poetry is an ongoing creation, open to alteration and improvement all the time. It may not have occurred to you to think in terms of a 'longer work' where poetry is concerned (as opposed to setting about a novel, or collection of short stories). But poetry collections are very often held together by a loosely connecting thread, e.g. a miscellaneous collection of love poems, or a sonnet sequence. Do you have a tale to tell? If it's going to end up fairly long, like so many famous epics it can come in the form of rhyming couplets, two successive lines of poetry that rhyme with each other, or alternating couplets, where alternate lines rhyme. Matching form to content is the secret, and finding a form that you're happy with.

Therapeutic poetry topics/themes

If you read poetry widely, both ancient and modern, you find certain themes that keep recurring. Some topics can be expressed very well in poetic form, and poets have continued to return to them in their writing regardless of style and approach. I have grouped some of these recurring themes under the following headings, and as you will see, overall topics/themes are broad and general in scope, the type of thing that can be widely interpreted by the prospective writer. The following list is not in any particular order.

1. *Time passing*: the ageing process; what's changed for better or worse – and what hasn't changed; death – one's own anticipated/ the loss of a loved one/grieving.
2. *Love poetry*: portrait of a loved one; love letters in verse; unrequited love; triangles; separation; lonely hearts.
3. *Celebrating Something Enjoyable*: playing or watching a sport; a thing of beauty admired; a view or landscape; nature, flora and fauna.
4. *Bemoaning Something*: relationships; chores; one's own shortcomings; the weather.
5. *Loneliness*: mental, physical and social effects.
6. *Happiness Concepts*: ask yourself what can/could make you happier and spend a poem answering that question (or several poems).
7. *Lifestyles*: one or more poems on alternative lifestyles that you would like to adopt (e.g. becoming a tramp or backpacker for a year; joining the Marines).
8. *Alternative Viewpoints*: examining your expectations and what you consider 'normal' by allowing that the opposite viewpoint may be valid; phobias and prejudices and what causes them (yours and other people's); 'wearing a different hat' – how do you see yourself in your different roles in life? Or have you only one role and would like to break free from it?
9. *Dreams and Ideals*: your ideal landscape/townscape/seascape; your ideal man/woman; 'Desert Island Thoughts'; political reform in verse!
10. *Dialogue in Poetry*: addressing someone or something and anticipating their reply; a serious or a light-hearted discussion.

Add to this list as ideas occur to you. The main thing about these 10 suggestions is that they should lead to more than one poem associated with each, and maybe even several that can be grouped under one heading to form a mini-collection.

Humorous poetry

Any of the suggestions in the previous section can have a thick coating of wit applied. Or you can set about the writing of humorous poetry simply to have fun and mess with words, for the purpose of lightening the spirits. Ask yourself a question (which can be either the poem's title, or its first line, or both) and spend the rest of your poem listing possible answers. Your conjectures can become as weird or bizarre as you like – or you can just ask unexpected questions and offer no answer, leaving it to your reader's imagination ("What would *you* do with a Wobbledewoo?").

You may decide that you're going to write, for instance, a nursery rhyme, and then come up with a subject – or do it the other way round by finding a subject and then deciding which treatment would suit it best. Or try inventing new words and then incorporate these into a poem (in the case of the Wobbledewoo just mentioned – ask yourself what it looks like? What is it used for? Does it make a noise? etc.) And in writing poetry purely for humorous purposes we can be as escapist as we like, asking 'what if …?' or completely redesigning something – or someone!

Exercises

Try any of the following in rhyming couplets (lines of poetry of similar length that rhyme):

1. *The Barbecue*: a pig family is having a barbecue (people burgers?) Think who you'd like to barbecue, e.g. any politicians; your mother-in-law; and allow them to be done to a turn by your pig family. What would you serve them with – French fries? Tangy barbecue sauce? And what are they going to taste like? (See also How-to poems, no.4 below).

2. *Design the Perfect Human Being*: you accidentally trigger the appearance of a fairy godmother who allows you this one wish – you can re-design yourself. Would you prefer a second pair of hands? A third leg? Telescopic vision? Supersonic hearing?

3. *'I Saw' Poems*: each line or each alternate line of the poem begins with the words 'I saw'. You are the disbelieving observer watching the spacecraft landing; you're a punter in the crowd cheering at a

dinosaur race; a child peeping through a hole in the fence at the weird old man or woman next door; or you're simply observing nature/the elements/birds/flowers behaving in 'an unaccustomed manner'. Think in terms of 'I couldn't believe my eyes' – and the occasions you've heard someone say that. What causes such astonishment? Very often something is much bigger than we expect; sometimes much smaller; or behaviour is unexpected/bizarre.

4. *'How-to' Poems*: a How-to poem is a set of instructions in poetry form, or directions to get from A to B. John Updike, for instance, in his poem 'Planting a Mailbox' uses the same tone as a gardening manual to instruct you how to plant your mailbox which will eventually blossom into a 'young post office'. The tone of a how-to poem is one of 'first do this, then do that', i.e. using the imperative to give commands to the reader. This area also includes recipes – for The Barbecue (no. 1 above) you could easily make this a how-to poem with instructions for using your barbecue to cook people, quantities to use, and 'method' as in any recipe instructions (you can borrow the terminology direct from any recipe book). Or you can offer advice: if this happens, you need to do that. The advice can be either a warning against dangers, or the best-way-to-do something sort of advice. You can even remonstrate with yourself after you've failed to follow your own advice: 'Well, I told you so …' .

5. *Questions*: why *did* that chicken cross the road? To teach its chicks road safety? Was it the chicken equivalent of a lollipop lady, outside a coop? A lot of nonsense poetry begins by asking a question, sometimes totally unlikely, but it can equally be a perfectly serious question with some very weird suggestions for answers.

> *"What would you do with a Wobbledewoo*
> *Colour it pink, or colour it blue?*
> *I'd like mine with a deepish, purplish hue*
> *And I want one that jumps like a kangaroo."*

6. *Conversations*: humorous verse is rich in conversations between frogs and toads, princes and princesses/frogs and princes, toads and princesses … and frequently inanimate objects acquire the ability to speak. A very useful form for having a good moan about something … and then telling yourself off for doing so!

87

Decide what to complain about, and in your first verse address it direct. In the second verse, you receive an unexpected reply – and the conversation continues either ending in an argument or reconciliation.

7. *Limericks*: the standard limerick format is 5 lines with a syllable-count of 9,9,6,6,9 or 10,10,7,7,10. The rhyme-scheme corresponds, being a,a,b,b,a. Usually those 5 lines are a 'one-off', and a collection of limericks will range over almost any humorous topic with each one being on a separate subject. But there's nothing to stop you using the limerick format for each verse in a longer poem. Don't forget to make your two line-ending rhymes easy to match for sound. Classic beginnings for a limerick are the words "There was a … from …" or "There once was a …". Either that, or plunge straight into a description of a hero or heroine, e.g.

> "*A psychotic street-walker from Ealing*
> *Went to consult a man about healing.*
> *At the sight of her glands*
> *He said "Don't mind my hands –*
> *I've decided you need your bumps feeling."*

Exercises

Try a limerick using one of the following as your first line:

- There was a footballer from Tooting …
- The Old Vic had a doorman called Hennery
- I once wandered lonely and cloudy
- A Gurkha sat high on an elephant

Accidents: several of the preceding suggestions for humorous poetry can result in an accident. Poetry about accidents often deals with horrendous choppings-up of people or oneself, accidental transporting to foreign parts, wrong buttons being pressed, and the opposite of what was intended being achieved. Try:

- "The Day I Faxed Myself/My Mum" (who to? Where did you/she end up? Did this open up endless possibilities for faxing people?)

- "The Wrong Parts": a mix-up happens in a hospital – tonsils are transplanted or swapped for adenoids, an appendix is mistaken for someone's nose replacement during cosmetic surgery …

Songs, spirituals and hymns

Poetry put to music? In Chapter 3, I dealt with music as a source of inspiration – listening to it, immersing yourself in it, and then describing the sounds in words. But we can use the terms 'songs' or 'hymns' to describe the type of *poem*, rather than having any music associated with it. A joyous celebration in verse may well be called a song or hymn, maybe even in its title, as Walt Whitman did in his epic-length *Song of Myself* (1855) which begins with the line *I celebrate myself*. Or as in the case of Edna St. Vincent Millay, her poem about funerals is entitled *Dirge Without Music* – a song or hymn doesn't have to be joyous in tone. Liz Lochhead's *The Empty Song* begins: *Today saw the last of my Spanish shampoo* which reminds her where she obtained it, who she was with, and the fact that their relationship has now ended.

If you think about the various topics that words put to music have covered over the years – love songs being just one sub-section – you can expect poetry written as a song to range over a similar breadth of topic. Often the glories of nature are the subject; folk ballads; heroic deeds. And some well-known poems have in fact had music put to them – William Blake's collection of *Songs of Experience* contains:

From Milton

And did those feet in ancient time
Walk upon England's mountains green?
And was the holy lamb of God
On England's pleasant pastures seen?

A *spiritual* is by dictionary definition and tradition 'a black American religious song', although for the purposes of poetry we can perhaps tone down the religious theme if wished – the 'sound of men working on the chain gang' appeals to the spirit or deals with suffering. Or a spiritual can be an outright celebration of God, in the same way as a *hymn* may be. The term hymn can however be used for any poem in praise of someone or something and may be adoring or glorifying in tone. *You'll Never Walk Alone* is now sung at football matches as a substitute hymn in praise and support of a team and managed to 'catch on' amongst the football-supporting public in spite of its lyric quality (where something more chant-like might have been expected).

So in order to write poetry that 'sings' in celebration – whether it be celebrating God or a football team – what do we need to consider?

- *A repeated refrain or chorus*: repetition is frequently a feature, either of a few words (i.e. a refrain as with the words *You'll Never Walk Alone*) or a whole chorus of two or more lines that is repeated after each separate verse. In doing the actual writing we therefore have to come up with something that will bear such repetition – a strong first line, for instance, or words so lyrical that the reader won't notice their repetition. And if you want your reader to have those words firmly embedded in their memory, they will need to be as simply memorable as *You'll Never Walk Alone* – nothing pompous, rarified, unpronounceable. If you're having trouble finding anything that will bear such repetition, it may well be sufficient to repeat the first verse, or couple of lines, at the end as a 'rounding-off'.

- *Rhyme, rhythm and beat*: no, it doesn't have to have any of these! In exactly the same way as any other form of poetry can come with a strict beat and rhyme-scheme or be totally free-flowing free verse, a song, hymn or spiritual can vary depending on subject-matter and your own preferences. To begin with, it *may* prove easier to structure your song via a firm beat and/or rhyme-scheme. But if, for instance, you've been able to produce two lines to use as a refrain which are of different lengths and don't rhyme, then follow those up with the body of your song in a similar mode, don't ever try and straitjacket words to fit a format when they're flowing nicely along different lines.

Exercises

(i) *A Song of Celebration*: have you any reason to celebrate one of the following? Choose a topic, and then write a song using either rhyming couplets, alternating couplets, or free verse, as you think fit:

- The advent of the computer and what it can do for you personally;
- A sporting event you either witnessed or took part in;
- A national, news-headline success of some sort;
- Reaching a milestone in your career/marriage.

(ii) *An Object of Worship*: do you have a particular object in your life that has special significance? This could be either religious, deeply spiritual, or emotional significance – a picture, photograph, ornament, old toy, piece of jewellery, a good-luck charm. What are the associations it conjures up, and does contemplating it give you increased energy, resolve or similar? Describe in song form the significance it has for you and how it makes you feel.

Banging your head against a brick wall

Poetry can bang its head where prose would give a good talking-to! Prose is simply too long and wordy sometimes to express frustration quite as effectively as a poem can. And for those who may not have a wide vocabulary at their fingertips, or for whom metaphor and simile may not spring easily to mind (to create a more 'elevated' style), poetry can use other ploys to great effect:

- *Repetition*: if you listen to a heated argument you'll find phrases or whole sentences repeated, as if to try and drum into someone's brain the point that's being made. Try starting every line of a poem with the same word or words, e.g.

  > "If you'd only listen ..."
  > "If I've told you once ..."
  > "If that's your attitude ..."

The pointing, stabbing finger of accusation or refutation can be illustrated verbally by repetition

> "I never said that,
> I never said nothing,

> *He's making it up,*
> *He's lying."*

Or perhaps you may prefer the resigned approach, which comes with the deep sigh of "here we go again":

> *"I told you streets weren't paved with gold,*
> *I told you so, but you didn't listen …"*

where frustration has grown weak with repetition.

In the case of frustration with an object rather than a person, you can even employ the opposite of a How-to poem (a 'How-Not-To' poem) where each sentence begins with 'I' doing something or having done something and still managing to fail against all the odds – 'I' did this, then I did that and then I did the other – but the thing still didn't work. What you can of course *then* do, on the page, is smash the thing to pieces and thoroughly enjoy doing so!

- *Graffiti:* rather than use a spray-can on a wall, can you say the same thing on a page? Take a standard graffito-message to use as your title and/or first line for a poem – and give someone a verbal thumping or put the world to rights. You can always alter the wording slightly. Some well-known suggestions:
- Prepare to meet thy doom
- Kilroy was here
- Jesus saves
- Make love not war
- … rules OK

Exercise: Conversation with a brick wall

What advice is the brick wall going to give you after you've either head-butted it or sprayed it with graffiti? Is it going to begin with a "Just who do you think you are" tone of voice, or politely ask if you'd mind not doing that again? Or perhaps it's addressing you before you've done anything, as you approach it? A warning-off, perhaps? We associate the term 'brick wall' with something or someone stubborn and immovable – can you give your brick wall just such characteristics as it responds to you and your behaviour? Perhaps it has a schoolmarmy manner, or a bossy policeman, or a thug: "Don't point your finger at me like that". Decide what your wall is going to represent for you-an obstacle you need to climb over or something that needs a sledge-hammer to knock it down? Or are you going to use your equivalent of a pen to be mightier than a sword – and spray it with poetry?

Conjuring up images (see also Chapter 3d)

(i) *Simile*: we conjure up images by the use of simile even when we're small children. In order to describe to a parent or teacher what something looks or sounds like, we use the words "it was like …" or "it was as … as …" – direct comparison. Poetry is full of similes, helping to create mood, atmosphere, and paint a picture. One of poetry's most famous images has Wordsworth in the Lake District wandering *'lonely as a cloud/that floats on high o'er vales and hills'* – a straightforward simile to convey how he feels. But many similes have unfortunately now been done to death (as dead as a dodo?). We use the phrase 'as blind as a bat' in everyday speech, for instance, so if we want to be original about someone's lack of sight we shall have to come up with something far more imaginative to insert in poetry. Shakespeare begins his Sonnet 18 with the famous line *'Shall I compare thee to a summer's day?'* to try and describe the object of his affections, so any of us using a summer's day as a simile will be accused of lack of originality. *'My love is like a red, red rose'* is the opening line of a song which may have been a fresh and interesting simile years ago when it was written – but due to over-use, roses have now become a hackneyed cliché. And we need to find alternatives to 'as white as a sheet', 'it dropped like a stone', or 'it shone like a diamond'.

So how to create original similes? It will depend on the tone of your poem whether you want to be weird and way-out, to shock the reader, or romantic and lyrical and need a soothing image:

does she walk like an angel playing a harp? (a comparison based on sound rather than the more obvious comparison with something visual). To create similes with a difference we need to go for the unexpected, to highlight what might otherwise go unnoticed, to compare an item from one realm with another item from a totally unrelated area, e.g. violent weather compared for sound with the instruments of an orchestra.

Exercise

Colours have been used for similes so often in poetry that making an original colour comparison that someone else hasn't already used is becoming more and more difficult. Can you take each colour of the rainbow in turn and create at least one simile of your own, using a comparison from an entirely different area? Keep your eyes open when out and about for unusual items whose colour fits the bill – rather than as red as a rose, can we have as red as a Liverpool football shirt? You can then use any similes that you're particularly happy with to contribute to Assignment 7 at the end of this chapter – does any one colour symbolise anything special for you?

(i) *Metaphor*: for the creation of metaphors we don't just compare something with something else – we *call* it by a new name. A smaller building next to a skyscraper is described as being 'dwarfed' by it – it hasn't turned into a dwarf, as this would imply, it's still a building, but we understand the size-comparison that's intended. Large hailstones are falling and we say it's 'coming down stair-rods' ... of course they're still hailstones, but the force and straightness with which they're falling gives the impression they're lengths of metal (as used by the Victorians to keep lengths of stair-carpet in place). Both of these examples are metaphors: if we were to say 'it's coming down *like* stair-rods', we'd have a simile.

Metaphor is used so much throughout poetry that we may not be aware of it, until a deliberate autopsy is undertaken to examine just which words constitute metaphors. Verbs are one area which is ripe with opportunities to use colourful, rich metaphors, and as poetry is always trying to convey a lot in a few words, one area you should deliberately cultivate is a good stock of such strong verbs.

Exercise

How many single-word alternatives can you find for the following? Add to your stock as you come across new ones.

* To go slowly (Example: we use the metaphor of cars in a traffic jam 'crawling')
* To go fast
* To talk loudly
* To talk quietly
* To be active
* To be inactive

Now can you insert any of the above verbs into a whole line of poetry, or several lines? Is there, for instance, anyone who springs to mind who always 'talks loudly'? Can you describe him/her in just a couple of lines, including your talk-metaphor?

(ii) *Onomatopoeia*: boom, tick, coo, burp, whirr! Onomatopoeic words like these have resulted from someone trying to put a noise on the page. In poetry, this is like adding the sound dimension to the visual after a picture has been painted so that we can also *hear* what's happening. You may have already used onomatopoeia in the Exercise above in order to convey someone talking loudly or talking quietly.

Exercise

Have a look back to Chapter 3(d), the exercise at the end. This list of verbs to do with rain was intended for a prose description here – but can you now do the same thing in poem form? Several of these words are onomatopoeic, and you may be able to come up with some more to reflect the noise rain makes (perhaps falling on different surfaces?)

(iii) *Symbols*: in Section 2 of Chapter 4, I began my section on Symbols by explaining that a symbol is an image endowed with meaning; it represents something to the beholder. We then went on to deal with personal objects and their meaning for us. But society as a whole has its symbols that have entered the national psyche: we associate doves with peace, fire with purging or cleansing, light with truth and the vision ahead, and the wind with a breath of life – and several civilisations have adopted these symbols, independently of each other, over time. Today, the advertising industry relies heavily on the use of symbols to convey images to the public as a whole: we see a pure white beach with palm trees and blue sky and are meant to think 'bliss' immediately, rather than to suppose there's a motorway just out of the picture, or a noisy holiday camp. In writing poetry, metaphor, simile and onomatopoeia can all be used to evoke images and symbols to help paint a picture we can make sense of: it will relate to something we're familiar with, even if that something is unpleasant.

Many symbols are established in the national psyche as representing what's acceptable/good/bad/unacceptable or frightening/friendly, e.g. a swastika represents fascism at its worst, whereas a Christian cross on a building indicates to us a haven of peace, tranquillity and safety. "In themselves, images, like objects, are meaningless; they acquire value only when we grant it to them … . Every culture has its symbol bank. The art of therapy is to render its resources accessible to the patient so as to provide a symbol transfusion …" (Anthony Stevens: *Private Myths* 1995, Penguin).

Assignment 7: Symbol bank

I mentioned the swastika and the Christian cross previously as examples of symbols in Western European culture. Can you think of others? Make a list for your own 'symbol bank', with notes about what significance they have, both for you personally and for society generally. Hopefully you will be able to refer to this list, not only for poetry-writing, but for other forms of writing you may try. Continue to add to it as ideas occur – and while doing so, consider which items you could use as metaphors?

8 Writing aids for the beginner

IN CHAPTER SEVEN I COVERED POETRY ideas and prompts, so this chapter is aimed mainly at prose-writing – although you may be able to use as a poetry subject a character created as a result of Section 2 of this chapter. There are many books to help you with the writing of prose fiction (short stories and novels), and also prose non-fiction (biography/autobiography; travel writing; magazine articles; etc.) or writing for radio and television. So this chapter is merely going to offer a few handy hints: if you want to learn more or specialise in one particular area, any library will have a selection of books for you to use.

Creating a storyline

1. You will find it easier to get things moving on the page if you've already done some *planning*. If you don't know where your storyline is going, how do you know when it's arrived? We usually associate the word 'plot' with something underhand and criminal, but for our purposes here I shall take it to mean the working-out of your storyline to achieve the ending you're aiming at. With something the length of a novel that can prove very difficult, and many a novelist sets out to tell a story not knowing where it will lead. But whatever the eventual length, you will make the writing easier if you have some sort of overview, even a vague end-in-view. So rather than plan a beginning, middle and then an end … how about starting with the end, then the beginning – and finally the complicated middle? This doesn't just apply to fiction: for auto-biography, for instance, you may well want to begin with the here and now, then flash back to childhood and work forward from there.

2. *Storyline Planning* will be made much easier if you can first decide *how much to tell* your reader or viewer. Think continually in terms

of what they *need* to know – and only tell them just enough so that they can follow the clues you're throwing in (in the case of crime fiction) or sufficient autobiographical detail, facts and figures so that they aren't overburdened by irrelevant details. This will probably involve you thinking back and re-reading what you've written to make sure all is logical and your reader or viewer can follow the gist. When it comes to plotting, you the writer are the all-knowing hand of God who can throw in red herrings, unexpected twists … and of course you already know whodunnit, who fancies whom secretly, and all the details of your characters' pasts! You may find yourself having to re-arrange the order of events for the benefit of the reader or viewer to make sure certain information is in place and everything is plausible – this applies to both fiction and non-fiction. Motives need to be viable and arguments legitimate. In order to drive home a point or plant a clue you may need to exaggerate, and equally you may want to play down some detail that proves to be vital, to keep them guessing.

3. *Premise*: apart from deciding how much your readers need to know to maintain interest in the storyline, you also have to decide just *how much they can be expected to know*. When writing for any audience or readership you will always have to bear in mind what information they can safely be expected to have at their fingertips, and how much you'll need to give them – or remind them. For instance, will they need reminding who was Prime Minister over the period you're referring to, or can you just throw in a name and expect everyone to recognise its importance? Will they remember that computers were not yet in general use during the period you're talking about? Do they know what oil-cloth is, or a doily, or a commode? etc. Always assume ignorance – you may have to drop hints to keep your reader in the picture (in the case of writing for TV, this is one area where the visual can do the job admirably by actually showing the item).

4. *Whose story is it*? Decide at the very outset whether to use the 'I' form, (the first person) or the 'he/she' form (the third person) – or are you going to be the all-seeing fly-on-the-wall narrator? Even if you're writing about yourself, you may still want to talk about yourself in the third person to give distance

and anonymity. If, perhaps, you're writing about a problem or past events from your own life, but have created fictional characters for this to happen to – whose viewpoint do you want to take? A third person such as a relative or neighbour, perhaps, and look at events through their eyes? Or a general onlooker such as the newspaper reader, who therefore ends up with the opinions the rest of the world will share of events? Or do you want to remain the omniscient narrator who can then show the discrepancy between what the world sees and what *really* happened? (With the latter you do get a more balanced viewpoint – but do you necessarily want that?)

5. *Problems and Choices*: the essence of plotting is to create a problem for someone, offer them choices as to how to solve it, and then show the outcome being worked out. Storytelling describes the process by which this happens. The 'choices' part might involve any of:

- To tell or not to tell? (about someone else, or whether to 'own up')
- Selective memory: who's remembered what; prejudice colouring the details;
- Fear: threat of violence/of being uncovered/of hurting someone;
- Embarrassment: e.g. because of a drunk-driving charge;
- How to overcome non-cooperation, e.g. anti-police feeling; medical ethics;
- Lack of evidence/uncertainty;
- Who's telling the truth? – false witnesses;
- Misunderstandings: how to interpret explanations and information;

6. *Time-chart*: this can prove a most useful aid for you to work out who did what and when, before deciding what to put in and what to leave out … and when you've decided what to include – in what order?

7. *Secrets*: in both fact and fiction, journalism and TV drama, secrets keep on recurring as an excellent basis for an intriguing plot, or an eternal point of interest for readers. People continue to have secret romantic affairs, to have their criminal pasts uncovered, etc.

Exercise: Secrets

Apart from the two secrets just mentioned in (seven) above, can you think of any more 'original' secrets, especially related to today's life-styles and events? Make a list, then pick out any in particular you think might prove a good basis for a fictional plot.

8. *Basic Plots*: there are several 'standard' plots that form the basis of much writing, e.g.

   - *Boy meets girl*, boy loses girl, boy regains girl;
   - *Rags to riches*: hero/heroine triumphs over poverty that (s)he's been born into;
   - *Overcoming adversity*: obstacle placed in way of progress – could be anything from physical deformity to a dragon, from bureaucracy to a mother-in-law!
   - *Riches to rags*: downfall of hero/heroine due to circumstance, accident or personality defects; has to learn either to be poor and happy or to regain riches with better insight;
   - *Rites of passage*: could be saga, over many years; or maturing of someone who has to learn about life in order to move on; or a critical period of change, e.g. puberty/leaving school/marriage/divorce/retirement/widow(er)hood.

   Everything from fairy tales to science fiction to soap operas all use these basic plots in some form or another.

9. *Sparking off a Storyline*: the basic plot list contains the essence of what a story may be about, but when you're faced with a blank page and are wondering where to begin to introduce your storyline, there are several ploys you can use:

   - *Ask yourself "what if ...?"* What if this were happening some time in the future or the past; what if it wasn't a man it was happening to, but a woman; what if the person were of a different race; what if the boot were on the other foot ... etc., etc.
   - *A snatch of conversation overheard* – e.g. a woman hears her husband's name mentioned making it clear he's been lying about his whereabouts;
   - *An incident witnessed* such as an attack or an accident;

- *A death*: not just for murder mysteries, but as a starting-point for biography, autobiography, a love story in retrospect;
- *A calendar date*: someone's birthday or anniversary; a memorial service; an appointment kept/not kept;
- *An object:* that sparks off memories; that is sent in the post; that appears in the back garden;
- *A meeting*: planned or unplanned – to start a love affair or instigate divorce proceedings? A wedding or a funeral, private party, etc.
- *A disappearance*: of a person or an object;
- *The unexpected*: someone acting totally out of character.
- *Response to an advertisement* is always a useful plotting device: you, the narrator, may have advertised in the 'Wanted' column for a particular object – a car, say, or an antique – or you need someone to work for you. Or you may be selling something in a For Sale column in the local press. What/who turns up in response to your advert? Or perhaps you are the respondent hoping to obtain a job or a bargain. What do you find when you get there?

Exercise: Lonely hearts

(a) You decide to advertise in the Lonely Hearts column of your local newspaper for some 'company'. Devise your advert, to make you as attractive as possible (while sticking to the whole truth!) Then write the responses you receive from

- Someone totally unsuitable
- Someone highly suitable
- Someone who's misunderstood what you're after.

Your response can come in letter form, or over the telephone – in which case, write the ensuing dialogue (and include your thoughts as this person speaks to you).

(b) You read an advert in your Lonely Hearts column from someone who sounds like your ideal partner, so you respond. Decide what your approach will be – e.g. "You've always needed me, I'm wonderful" 'or' very apologetic for troubling you, but … .

After writing the first letter/making the first phone call and arranging to meet them, describe the meeting and what you find.

(c) You are the third-person narrator describing various responses to an advertisement in a Lonely Hearts column. You will need to work out first who it is who's advertised, their age, reason for advertising, etc. Then describe the various likely respondents. For each of these, you should be able to spark off a separate 'short' short story in itself – each respondent has a tale to tell/a reason for responding.

For any of the above (choices a, b or c) you may well be able to include as part of your storyline one or more of the secrets you came up with in the last exercise (under no. seven) – e.g. someone has advertised or responded who does in fact already have a partner, or is a wife-beater/child-abuser/just out of prison/etc.

Creating characters

In the previous section we examined under no.4 'Whose story is it?', to try and decide the point of view events are to be seen from. For a single short story you can only have a single narrator; but something to bear in mind is that events seen by someone else may look very different, and writers in the past have created a collection of short stories with the same basic events viewed by a different person for each story. Someone who appears a hero from one angle may be a villain seen from a different viewpoint. A writer may not even sympathise with the angle he or she is presenting events from, but will have to try and put aside personal prejudices and preconceptions in order to create a convincing character. You need to probe what makes a person tick, even if you don't like the sound of that tick.

1. *One principal character*, or several? Do you want a hero, heroine *and* a villain all sharing the limelight? In the case of non-fiction such as autobiography, or 'faction' where you're using life story with added characters or names, dates and places altered, you may well have this dilemma sorted out automatically. For instance, one of your parents could well be the 'hero' or 'heroine' with the other parent being the villain (or you the narrator as a rebellious teenage 'villain'?)

When you start to write, it will obviously entail less difficulty to keep things simple by having one main character, and the rest – the subsidiary characters – on the periphery, who only need mentioning in passing. There is always a danger, when using those around you on which to base your characters, of going into too much detail and recording e.g. your grandparents' schooldays or a neighbour's work history, which will detract from your storyline. Better to go into great detail about one main character and give the rest only walk-on parts.

In the case of a love story it may be difficult to give one half of the pair the principal role: they may share it equally. But more than two becomes a crowd where principal characters are concerned: even in a film like *The Magnificent Seven*, where a 'gang' of seven men are featured, they don't all get equal treatment – one or two are singled out as the main protagonists. So if you are dealing with a large family or a group of people where there's a temptation to try and be fair to everyone and give them equal writing space – don't! Take one person and look at him or her in the context of those around them, i.e. follow *their* storyline. Only with something as lengthy as a family saga, which will cover several generations, will you end up with more than one main character, one for each generation, and their stories will have to be skilfully welded together.

2. *Creating a Main Character*: when deciding viewpoint strategy, decide also who you want your readers to sympathise with. That person will then automatically be your main character. It may not be the apparent 'hero' or 'heroine' as far as the action is concerned, but could in fact be the person portrayed as the 'villain' with whom we sympathise.

In trying to draw up characteristics to give your main character, it's often better to make them an amalgam of features that will suit the plan of your story, rather than take a real-life person and build a story round them. You may well need someone who is sufficiently complex a character to act unexpectedly or to have a dark secret, rather than being clear-cut.

Many writers, both of fiction and biography, take the trouble to work out a *character profile* for main characters. This will include not just age, physical features, family background and relationships, but also how this person thinks, the sort of clothes they'd choose, ambitions, temperament, preferences in music, food, holidays, etc. Try to reach the stage where you can say with assurance to yourself "he'd never act like that" or "she'd never wear that type of thing", – because you know this person so well.

3. *Subsidiary Characters*: you'll still need to do some of the above character-profiling for those around your main character who feature in your writing, but not in so much detail. And at the bottom end of the character-importance scale will be people designed for only one purpose: to get the storyline moving, or help it along. Many a murder mystery has a body whose history we discover as the plot unfolds – but we only learn what's relevant to help the detective catch the murderer, and we'll never find out more than a few oddments about how that person thought, their tastes, etc. (we may learn no more than that he had big feet and had been an amateur boxer). This relates back to plotting, where I stressed that you only tell the reader what they *need* to know.

Since many a subsidiary character is only used for one particular reason, it becomes more difficult to try to portray them as real people when all they make is such a brief appearance. The danger is that they become caricatures, only there to represent one thing – "the bully" walks on at the beginning to bash someone up and cause the chip on their shoulder, but may play no further part. So a little more development is needed, to try to explain why this person became such a bully, and put him or her in context. Equally, fairy godmothers should not appear to solve your plot problems (unless in a fairy story!). Don't expect your readers to believe the sudden appearance towards the end of a rich uncle who will solve all money problems. If something like this is going to happen, it needs to be totally plausible and to have had clues planted much earlier in the story. A lottery win may pay off all debts in one go, but we need to have been told that the main character has been doing the lottery regularly for weeks and pinning hopes on it.

One form of subsidiary character who does have more durability, and more importance in basic plotting, is the *sidekick*. Not only detectives such as Holmes have a Watson, or Morse a Sergeant Lewis, but film heroes frequently team up with someone else (not necessarily of the same sex). Sidekicks perform a very useful characterisation function in that they're not usually as bright/heroic/athletic/etc. as their senior partner, so serve to highlight heroic qualities. But plot-wise they may be able to make discoveries in the absence of the hero/heroine, or point out alternative choices or motives. They serve as a sounding-board for the hero/heroine to bounce ideas off and for you the writer to ensure that your readers are aware of both sides of an argument.

Exercise

Have you any sidekick experience from real life? Have you ever been close friends with someone, or had a brother or sister, who always instigated the action/made decisions? Or have you had a close friend or relative who was content to let you do all the decision-making? If the latter, did you consider yourself the hero(ine) or leader and the other person your 'sidekick'? Describe the relationship – or a similar one that you've observed if it hasn't happened to you personally. Can you think of any particular incident that typified how the relationship worked, to include in your description?

4. *Baddies and Villains*: as we've already discovered, a *lovable* villain can become a hero ... but a true baddy will always have to play second fiddle to a hero(ine) – good must triumph! But we do need as much time, energy and skill devoted to portraying a sinister character effectively as we do for a main character, in order for them not to end up a caricature or stereotype. 'Baddy' stereotypes include the bully, someone blindly out for revenge, the mentally ill (e.g. schizophrenic), the selfish spoilt brat, the vindictive gossipy neighbour, the sexually unstable, the over-ambitious politician, the greedy businessperson. It's not enough – even if you're basing your baddy on someone from real life – to describe their actions and effect on the main character. We need to know *motives*: jealousy, for instance, or self-interest, insecurity, revenge or obsession. People aren't born bullies: explore what has made someone that way.

Then ask yourself about their *behaviour*: do they manage always to appear to the rest of the world as perfectly normal (but you the writer know different)? If someone is plotting revenge, we need hints early on that that's the way things are going. And is your baddy the open, up-front aggressive type or liable to under-hand tactics such as malicious phone calls or spreading false rumours?

Exercise: Appearances can be deceptive

Think of any situations you've been involved in or been told about/ read about where someone's evil intentions have been well-screened and people have been taken in. Now write up events as if you were doing a newspaper or local radio report. End with a warning as to what to look out for, what action to take and how to treat this person.

5. *Stereotypes*: as a nation, we have a nasty habit of stereotyping other nationalities: comedians use this to great effect for their jokes, automatically making anyone from the Far East talk in a 'ying-tong' voice, Americans wear stetsons, Scandinavians be tall and blonde. But closer to home we allow our prejudices to col-our our views of the opposite sex, people from another part of the country or a different social class, turning them into stere-otypes. And we expect certain people to look a certain way and will react accordingly: "Well, he *looks* like a yob", tending to justify the fact that we're treating him as if he were one. Hearing a voice down a telephone for the first time we gain an impression of what we expect that person to be like. From what they say we make assumptions about them – they 'sound like one of us' or share our views, or they're not someone we'd like to meet having heard them talk.

Exercises

(a) Are you guilty of letting your prejudices affect your judgement of other people? Have you ever been pleasantly/unpleasantly surprised upon meeting someone for the first time, when they turned out to be not what you'd expected? Use this experience to write up a fictional scene (either as narrative, or in dialogue for a radio or TV script), highlighting how preconceived ideas colour our judgement.

(b) *Portrait of an Angry Young Man*: a 'photofit' in words that typifies how you think of an angry young man. How would this person talk/think/dress/behave?

(c) *The Good, the Bad and the Ugly*: which film or TV hero or heroine do you particularly like or admire, and why? And which do you particularly hate, and why? Write a critique analysing what it is about the way the character is portrayed that either attracts or repels you (e.g. speech; appearance).

6. *Characterisation Aids*: when drawing up a character, whether based on real-life or purely fictional, you will need to describe the following for your reader:

(a) *Body language*: does this person make eye-contact, or is he/she a shifty-eyed type? Is their body posture aggressive, upright, sexy, submissive? Do they have any repeated gestures – clenching hands, hand-wringing, pointing, for instance? And facial expressions: always smiling? A down-turned mouth making them always look peevish? An eye-twitch? Think how they'd be standing or sitting at any one particular time – slumped over a chair, relaxing to watch TV, or in an interview room. Your reader needs to know if this person picks his/her nose, has hiccups, winks knowingly, or points. And we already associate noses with character traits – we talk about someone who's a snob having 'their nose in the air' or someone wrinkling their nose in disgust. We can have a character saying one thing while their body language says something different, giving away their real intentions.

(b) *Taste*: think what sort of music this character would listen to; what type of food he/she eats – micro-waved or home-cooked? A curry or fish and chips? What are his/her hobbies? (a couch potato or exercise freak? Chess champion or pigeon-fancier?) And we can always use clothing to make a statement about a character: a lot of the time we wear what's expected of us, e.g. to work or to a funeral. But to help

107

characterise a rebel, for instance, we can describe them wearing something totally *unexpected*.

(c) *Speech*: how does a character talk? Local accent, foreign accent, public school? Slurred due to drink? A speech impediment, breathlessness, quietly-spoken? Using the latest teenage buzz-words? How educated a person is will be reflected in their choice of vocabulary, but also how often they repeat themselves. The less well-educated tend to use shorter words and shorter sentences, and to swear a lot more. However, anyone can have their particular pet phrases that keep recurring. And anyone can 'rabbit on' at length or be tight-lipped in the amount of talking they do – what does this reflect? Are they a good listener, or do they continually interrupt and want to be heard?

When writing *dialogue* for insertion in prose, remember that natural everyday speech needs editing for the page – eliminate most of those ums and ers and repetition (but not all – you still want it to sound natural). Don't attempt a local accent unless you're completely familiar with it, and even then, your reader probably won't be, so just use it to 'flavour' your writing – in the same way as listening to a strong accent can become tiresome, so can having to read it. You can always say "… he said in his strong Cornish accent" rather than trying to spell out what he actually said.

Very often one character in a conversation is dominant, such as the interviewer interrogating the interviewee or the shopkeeper asking what the shopper would like and then explaining what's available.

Exercise: "What time do you call this?"

A daughter is creeping back into her home at 3.00 a.m. hoping not to disturb her parents. On the landing she encounters her irate father. Write the ensuing dialogue, including the body language of both parent and offspring in the narrative, their appearances, and including the odd word that will indicate the generation gap.

Scene-setting

A precise description of where a person lives, both locality and the type of accommodation, serves several purposes:

- *To give credibility* and make a place 'real';
- *As an aid to characterisation* – we can soon learn from the type of house/furniture/garden what sort of person lives there, and from the cleanliness of the streets, the sort of shops, the amount and type of traffic, the state of the public parks and buildings, what sort of a community this is;
- *As an historical record* of e.g. the economics of the country or of that locality at that time: still post-war bomb sites, or is there a lot of new building going on?
- *To indicate trends in society* e.g. a high street with empty shops but a thriving out-of-town shopping complex with huge car park; inner-city walls decorated with graffiti;
- *To reflect the mood of the times* – what does a 'depressed area' look like, and how does it make you feel? And leafy suburbs?

1. *Mood and Atmosphere*: simply driving into a town or city for the first time, or entering it by train, we pass from suburbs to the inner city or town centre and can soon gain an impression of the area and the people who live there. Drab and dirty buildings, boarded-up council estates, tatty old cars (and people) leave us with no doubt as to what sort of area this is. Equally, tidy rows of semi-detached houses with camper vans in their drives, followed by a medieval town square with the odd thatched roof housing a coffee shop, smell of money and loving restoration.

    The same applies when we walk into a public building, or someone's home – whoever's been in there will have left their mark in some way, whether it be careful preservation or untidiness. The mood and atmosphere of a place can be made vivid not just by describing what the eye sees, but also what we *hear* and *smell* – the flavour of the place. Does this church have a hallowed echo of footsteps on flagstones, or a fusty dusty smell to it? Is this house thick with stale cigarette smoke – or equally thick with air-freshener? Outside in the street, can we detect the local factory's output because 'the wind's in the wrong direction' – or is there a stiff salt sea breeze reaching us? On this housing estate is there a continual blast of pop music from radios – or the buzz of lawn-mowers?

What many of us think of as repellent may have a special place in your affections, or the affections of someone close to you. On meeting Marion from the Australian suburbs who was over here visiting the UK, I was relating how post-war pre-fabricated housing was used to solve that immediate housing problem, but that some of it had survived for years, and how ugly it was with its corrugated iron roofing. Marion's reaction was to relate her affection for a corrugated iron roof, and the sound of rain on it, as remembered from her childhood, which had given comfort for falling asleep. Once our affections have become attached to a place, or an aspect of that place, our view of it will always be coloured by emotion.

Exercise

How do you feel about the area you grew up in? Did you want to get out of it as soon as you could, or does it to this day bear a special place in your affections? What was there about the overall mood and atmosphere of the place that made you love/hate it? Or was it just plain boring? Describe it for someone who's never been there, and recommend them either to visit it – or not, as the case may be.

2. *Landscape painting* (also townscapes and seascapes): you will have to decide for yourself just how detailed you want to be when describing a landscape, but even a few spare 'brush strokes' in words will create an impression of a view. Choose a few salient features to pick out, or 'highlight' as a painter would, and describe these in more detail than the rest of the surroundings. The features you choose should be representative of the area – a factory chimney and some engine sheds; an office block and a Victorian bank building; a row of detached individually-designed homes with large gardens; the pier and the promenade; the village post office and the manor house. Use your description to reflect the community in which these items are situated – usually because they're totally typical, but it could also be because they stand

out like a sore thumb from the rest of their surroundings. Is this because someone came along and decided to stamp their individuality on the area in the past, creating what we call a 'folly'? Or the modern-day townscape equivalent – where someone has purchased their council house and altered its frontage, making it stand out from the rest of the row?

Exercises

(a) *Figure in a Landscape/Townscape*: is there anyone you know/have known whom you associate with a particular landscape? This could be anyone from a man on his allotment to a farmer in his fields; a woman on a bicycle; two teenagers in an empty car park; a scavenger on the local tip; or a street sweeper. Describe the landscape or townscape and the person in relation to it: are they perfectly at home here and never likely to leave, or just biding time before they can get out?

(b) *The View from my Window*: take one particular window – could be from your place of work, a hospital window, or home – and describe the view from it. This could be a roofscape – do the types of roof reflect the area? Don't limit your view to the immediate garden or car-park, but look further to the overall scape. Is this an area you want to be living or working in? How do you feel about it?

3. *Exterior Design*: we all have our ideas about the ideal type of house we'd like to live in, and what sort of public buildings we want to see in our towns and cities. What might have seemed an austere Victorian heap of a building can come to be regarded with respect, if not affection, once we've worked or lived in it and have accumulated memories associated with it: it may not be ideal but once you've 'done time' in there, you become attached. The opposite is also true – in the case of 'doing time', a prison building can come to represent a nightmare, or the appearance of a hospital block to mean pain and death to one's memory. For describing the exteriors of buildings, here is a check-list of oddments for you to consider:

• *Colour and texture*: are we on a red-brick campus or in a concrete jungle?

- *How have the buildings weathered?* – matured, or fallen apart? Do they appear very different seen at a different time of day or year, in sunshine or in rain?
- *What are the immediate surroundings like?* – trees and gardens all round? And how old are they – mature, or saplings? Is there a park opposite, and what does it contain?
- *Sounds*: is this building within ear-shot of heavy traffic or docklands, for instance? Is it a haven of peace and quiet within, but noisy outside (or the opposite)?
- *Nature at work*: birds on the roof? Weeds in its cracks? Hanging baskets?

Exercises

(a) *Public Buildings*: is there one public building that you particularly love or hate? This could be anything from a school or library to a department store, a pub, church, hotel, village hall or town hall. Describe how you feel as you approach it: what you see, and what memories it conjures up.

(b) *Ideal Home*: what would your ideal home look like? A cottage by the sea, or a country mansion? Think not only of what you'd want it built of, but the wider ideal landscape you'd put it in. Do you want acres of garden, a swimming pool and stables? How *old* would it be – 300 years of history attached, or brand new architect-designed? Work out your specifications, then put in a written order to the great house-builder in the sky.

4. *Interior Design*

(a) *Private Interiors* – A catalogue of items viewed as the eye strays round a room can tell us quite a lot about who lives there, as well as décor and interior design that reflect personality, so in order to discover the 'sound' of the person living in the house or flat you're describing, ask yourself the following:

- Old-fashioned, or newly-decorated?
- Décor flamboyant or sedate? Tasteful or tasteless?

- Is it tidy/regimented/disorganised/a wreck?
- What type of pictures and ornaments are there? Kitsch bought at the local market, or expensive foreign artefacts?
- Has any one individual stamped themselves on this interior, or could it represent a thousand similar homes?
- Space and light, or dull, dingy and cramped?

And as with exterior design, always bear in mind noises, smells – and the view from the window(s).

Exercise: "My favourite room"

What makes you at home in this particular room? Describe it in the light of the above check-list, adding any more of your own considerations you can think of. Don't forget to include those similes, metaphors, onomatopoeia, etc. to paint a picture.

(b) *Public Interiors*: Moving from the individual and where he or she lives, public interiors have *lots* of people affecting the way the place looks, sounds and smells. A public library today may be a quiet haven or can have a noisy children's book corner to it. And if you want to describe what it's like entering Wembley Stadium for a cup final match – where to start? Rather than too many intimate details, as we've just had for private interiors, I'd refer you back to the Mood and Atmosphere section : an overall impression is needed. The same would apply for an art gallery – don't try and describe in detail every painting that's in there, but tell us e.g. what the place *sounds* like (does it have high ceilings that make your footsteps echo?)

Exercise

Following exercise 3(a), which was the outside of a public build-ing, can you now take us inside and describe what we find? Use the previous check-list as a basis for the sort of thing our senses will take in.

Factual sources

For non-fiction writing we need to have our facts right – dates, places, names. For fiction, we need them to *sound* right. That means highly likely for the time and place in which someone is living, for their social background, family, etc. We don't expect a Victorian housemaid to be called Charlene, nor do we expect a 1990s toddler to be called Ethel.

1. *Names*: before we even meet a person or visit a street, we get some sort of idea of what to expect from the name. If I tell you an address is Bismarck Street, off Victoria Square – how old would you expect the buildings to be? The fact that we're talking 'street' and 'square' immediately locates us in a town or city centre. On the other hand, The Cottage, The Green, Old Ellerby is definitely in rural England, whilst obviously *Ty Celyn* must be in Wales and *Waipapa* in New Zealand! And Back Market Lane could be in a city or a market town … but it will certainly be old, possibly dating back to medieval times. When you read 'lane', what do you expect to find? A narrow winding road with no room to pass, blind bends, and hardly a straight section? We have a choice, when searching for fictional names to use, of Lane, Walk, Road, Avenue, Street, Grove, etc.

   Choosing fictional names to give our characters means we can develop characterisation: if we discover a man is called Sidney, Cyril or Alf – do we expect to meet a teenager? (Unless we're dating action pre-war, we don't). If he's called Peregrine d'Arcy-Smith do we expect to meet a skinhead? Should you deliberately want to delude your reader you can of course use such a name for your skinhead – but then what's his background? Names change with time and fashion, and vary according to social class, so always have a good think before naming your characters and ask yourself "from that background and of that age, would he/she really be called that?"

   Foreign names, also, need to be spelt realistically so some research may be needed. The phone book may suffice for surnames, or you can borrow a well-known surname (e.g. Polanski; Ishiguro; Biedermeier) – but then it may well need a suitable matching fore-name (plus a name for other members of the family). City archives have records from censuses, births, marriages and deaths, going back centuries, so have a quick look here to spot recurring family names for the area. Or you can use their old newspaper copies and see what were typical names for people being arrested/robbed/becoming politicians/dying during the period you're interested in.

Exercises

(a) Describe what you'd expect the following to look like, what sort of age are the buildings, and what part of the city, town or village are we in? Allow a short paragraph for each.

- Elm Tree Avenue
- Waterworks Lane
- Chetwynd's Alley
- Smithy Street
- Oil Sites Road
- Cherry Walk
- Jubilee Square

(b) From the following names, can you compile a brief character outline? (3 or 4 sentences)

- Ada Cowton
- Derek Wilson
- Mark O'Grady
- Victoria Montague
- Cheryl Smith
- Albert Biggins

2. *Visual Illustration*: something that the prospective reader of non-fiction will expect to see, whether they're opening a history book or a biography, *Tales from Turkmenistan* and *The Complete guide to Cabinet Making*, is illustration. This can take the form of photographs, diagrams, maps, charts, newspaper cuttings – anything that helps to clarify or expand upon the text. If you're writing up your life story, or someone else's, have you a store of

photographs? In order to use these with any sort of authority, you'll need to know exactly who is portrayed (if your subject is in the middle of a family group, for instance – but not for a whole school classful!) The date it was taken, and the location, are equally necessary, and for newspaper cuttings, the date the paper was published. A family tree will help enormously to put people in context with each other, and a street map will put that family in the context of their community/locality.

If you have these available to use, they can form a very useful basis from which to begin writing as they will inevitably spark memories. Apart from explaining to a reader – or simply to remind yourself – where and when the photo was taken or the newspaper article written, ask yourself:

- What *personal event* did this record? A holiday, birthday party, marriage or anniversary?
- What *national events* were going on at the time?
- For a photo, how were you *feeling* at the time? Bored silly, or was this the greatest day of your life?
- If we can see *other people, buildings or landscape* in the background, who or what are they? Put this photo in context.
- For *an article*, was this newspaper the local rag? What sort of quality was it, how long had it been produced?
- *What happened next?* (for both photos and article cuttings)

Assignment 8: Creating a portfolio

You can use the various pieces of writing resulting from exercises in this chapter as the basis for a portfolio. In writing terms, a portfolio is a collection of examples of what you've written, not necessarily finished pieces. It could contain just a few sentences on one topic, but these 'snippets' can be used for expansion later. Also include notes made, extracts cut out, ideas jotted down. Start collecting written items such as your character sketches, landscape sketches in words, rooms described, photographs and cuttings that you think you may be able to use. Include in the latter cut-out photos of interesting faces you can use as a basis for creating characters. This 'portfolio of faces' doesn't need details about their background, age, etc. – it's the interesting face that you will use. Observe behaviour, body-language, clothing and appearances and note these down; do the same for any names you spot, and file these according to age and social class – you may even be able to match these up with some of your photo-cuttings to create a fictional character in writing. Your portfolio should eventually become a treasure-trove of bits and pieces you can draw on.

9 Projects and assignments

SO FAR IN THIS BOOK THE majority of the exercises have been short, one-off pieces of writing that could either stand on their own or be saved to add up to something bigger. The assignments at the end of each chapter are intended to be 'something bigger', with hints and suggestions as to how this might be achieved. In this chapter you will find more of the latter – topics for projects that can diversify into different areas, and assignment follow-ups. These should set you thinking first, rather than be used merely to practise one aspect of writing. Hopefully by now, after a choice of 55 exercises in chapters 1–8, you will have managed to make a start with some writing of some sort. Until now it has been a matter of getting that pen or computer moving: now for the serious stuff!

1. *Assignment 1 Follow-Up – Learning Diary*
   If you've been keeping notes while reading this book as suggested at the end of Chapter 1, can you now turn these into a Review of Progress? Include the following areas:

   - How much writing have you achieved? Make a catalogue.
   - Do you want to continue, or have you had enough? Try to explain why.
   - Even if you don't want to continue, can you assess how much use (if any) attempting writing has been? E.g. did it help you to get something off your chest?
   - Decide *which sort of writing* came easiest: autobiography (e.g. anecdotes from real life), fiction (creating characters and places) or perhaps poetry? Why do you think that was – and was it what you expected, or did you surprise yourself?
   - Which *aspect* of the writing process was hardest? E.g. starting from scratch with a blank page – or did you suffer from writer's block once you'd got going? Was it difficult to be honest with yourself? Did you have trouble admitting things?

- Where to from here? Have you discovered an area that you definitely want to follow up on, and if so, why that area?
- Do you now feel confident enough to share what you've written with anyone else? If so, under what circumstances – e.g. is a writing workshop now a possibility? If anyone else has read what you've written, what was their reaction? And how did you feel about their response?

2. *Assignment 3 Follow-Up: Joy List*

   If you've managed to make any Joy List notes following Assignment 3, either as part of your Learning Diary or separately, can you now enlarge on these to form a magazine-style article? Go further back in time and list any positive high points as far back as you can remember. Your notes will obviously be highly autobiographical and could well represent a list of high points with no apparent connection. Assume you're going to save the article and re-read it in several years' time: what will you have forgotten? Think what sort of details you'll need to put the high points of your Joy List into some sort of context, e.g. where were you, who were you with, what year/season/day was it. You will then need to insert connecting sentences – which could gloss over days, weeks, months or even, in the case of thinking back to childhood, years, e.g. "I didn't have another day as enjoyable as that one until four years later, when …". There's a strong temptation to assume that because we can remember something clearly at the time of writing, we don't need to note it down, whereas in fact several years hence all may well be forgotten.

   It may prove easier to write – and more coherent – if you have a connecting thread such as your relationship with one person or place, and the high points associated with them. But there may be too few of these to create more than one paragraph. If so, have you a personal connecting thread, e.g. overcoming depression or illness, to use as the basic standpoint? It may have been – and still be – an uphill struggle … but nevertheless were there no brighter moments?

3. *Assignment Seven Follow-Up: Symbols*

   Did you manage to begin a Symbol Bank, as suggested in Assignment seven? So far, the exercises involving symbols in this book have been about thinking up and collecting symbols that mean something to you – or to the nation as a whole. We shall now look at how best to use your personal symbols in writing.

Inevitably, we all have symbols in our everyday lives that are full of negative associations: my mother was an arachnophobe, so anything looking vaguely like a spider or its web was a no-go area. You may well have already listed similar negative symbols that loom large in your mind when you're asked to think about metaphors, for instance. In order to use symbols effectively for therapy purposes, however, – forget the negatives and accentuate the positives! Think up symbols that only have good vibes for you, and ask yourself why they've come to represent good aspects of life? Is there, for instance, one piece of music that you associate with a loved one ("our song")? Or a trophy obtained due to great personal effort, that meant you had to discipline yourself to train mind or body (or that someone close to you managed to achieve), which will always be an object of pride? Perhaps you succeeded in making something by hand, against all the odds, or growing something in a garden?

In order to demonstrate in writing how a particular symbol gained its significance, can you now use it as the centre-point for a short story … or even a collection of short stories? One example of the latter – a single symbol being used repeatedly as the connecting thread for different stories – is the Holy Grail. King Arthur's knights went on a variety of quests for the elusive Grail, which loomed symbolically over their searches, and it has been used in literature repeatedly over time. In both adults' and children's literature, films and TV, we continue to find some symbolic object having to be sought, or rescued and returned to its rightful place/owner either because of its emotional significance, or simply to restore order and sanity to an otherwise chaotic world.

To help you transfer your chosen symbol into short story form, here are various ideas as to how you might use it:

- Assume it has been stolen, and base your story on its retrieval;
- Decide who you might give it to as a reward, and under what circumstances?

- You have left instructions in your will as to who should inherit this item: enclose with it a note to the receiver explaining what it meant to you, and why you're leaving it to them specifically;
- Any or all of the above ideas can be applied to *Fairy Tales*: in a fairy tale, a rose is never merely a rose but will have taken on some sort of symbolic significance, such as to represent the love between hero and heroine. Frequently, before the hero can win his beloved, he will have to undergo various feats – such as retrieving a missing object, killing a monster, crossing unmarked treacherous terrain, etc. Can you now design a hero, and show him handling setbacks and overcoming all odds to obtain the item that will win him his heroine? In a fairy-tale world, what would you find most off-putting – obstacles or people? Or both?
- Tribal myths over centuries have developed their *fertility symbols*, often using an item from their local environment (e.g a rock, tree or particular plant). Choose a symbol for a mythical couple to employ – have they perhaps produced nothing but daughters and want a son? If the symbol works and they do get a son, does he prove to be a ne'er-do-well – and what should we deduce from this?

4. *Parables and Allegories*

In Chapter 4 I mentioned parables under the heading "Humour", as a ploy to lighten a serious subject. That was just one use for them, but far more frequently they are a serious literary form.

If you find it difficult to divulge your thoughts and emotions on a page by using the 'I' form, or even the 'he' or 'she' version, there is a third option you might like to consider. We can 'depersonalise' experiences by turning them into a parable or allegory. A parable is "a story told to illustrate some doctrine or moral point" (Chambers Dictionary); allegory is "symbolical narration" – "an extended metaphor in which characters, objects, incidents, and descriptions carry one or more sets of fully developed meanings in addition to the apparent and literal ones. John Bunyan's *Pilgrim's Progress*, for example, is apparently about a man named Christian who ... 'stands for any Christian man, and the incidents of his journey represent the temptations and trials that beset any Christian man throughout his life on earth." (Reader's Encyclopedia).

A parable or allegory can be a 'model' case, an example or set of details amalgamated to illustrate the point you wish to make. The characters used in such a story will be there not as individuals struggling with a personal problem but as representatives of mankind/womankind facing the sort of problem we humans may all have to face at some time.

It may be possible when reading either parable or allegory to make exact identification between what is described and what it's supposed to represent (as in *Pilgrim's Progress*). Many modern short stories that fall into this category, however, use distortion, the absurd and the grotesque rather than a logical correlation, in order to stress a point. The opposing of officialdom and bureaucracy, for instance, can be very effectively demonstrated by someone representing the public in general trying to communicate with bureaucrats using perfect logic but finding themselves up against what appears to be an alien from another planet who speaks nothing but officialese. What follows may then defy all logic as frustration turns someone into a monster and we enter a sci-fi world. The Czech-born German writer Franz Kafka, in his famous short story *The Metamorphosis*, has his hero waking up one morning to find himself turned into a large beetle. The reader is invited, by the very absurdity of the situation, to work out what this could possibly represent. Obviously an allegory of some sort – but what? Various interpretations have been put on it, social and religious, in keeping with Kafka's themes of family life and man's relationship with God.

When it comes to writing a short story in parable or allegory form, you are able to do away with a lot of the individual characterisation that fiction normally demands: your characters are *representatives*, not individuals. So we can talk about 'the boy', 'the man', 'the old woman', 'the blacksmith' in an impersonal way, rather than invite readers to become involved emotionally with people, to sympathise or hate a character. Instead, we need to ensure that readers will think seriously about what characters are there to represent, and decide for themselves how to interpret facts and events. Very often with an absurd or grotesque theme, a factual, detailed, reportage style of writing is used to emphasise the discrepancy between everyday mundane life and what's really going on in someone's mind, or between what society is protesting openly and what it's really getting up to in private.

Project: "A Mental Pilgrimage"

People with incurable diseases may make a pilgrimage to a particular place, e.g. Lourdes, in the belief that the aura/historical or religious significance/waters there will assist healing and assuage pain. Mentally, we can make a pilgrimage for the same purpose: is there a particular place in your past, a particular house or building, a garden, a beach or a beauty spot in the countryside, which has soothing and healing memories for you? Describe the spot in physical detail, through the eyes of a pilgrim seeing it for the first time, using parable-style. Your characters, for instance, could well include 'the pilgrim', 'the priest', 'the physician', 'the nun', or 'the good companion'. You can then keep this description and 'make a pilgrimage' back there for your own purposes, when under stress or emotionally upset (you may even have a photo to accompany your writing?)

5. *Tribes*

For thousands of years our ancestors moved around in tribal groups, a sort of mobile extended family. For the individual within that tribe, there was always the certainty of 'back-up' – support in confrontations with other tribes, assistance to perform tasks, and the assurance of having around you people whose philosophic, moral and religious thinking was along the same lines. Over the last century we've seen the increasing break-up of the family – but mankind still needs to belong somewhere, to adhere to a unit that can give similar support to that provided by a tribe.

The modern-day version of a tribe may be anything from football supporters to the Women's Institute, a stamp collectors' club to the Freemasons, or the Ramblers' Association to the Seventh Day Adventists ... anywhere that people gather to form an identifiable group. What used to be tribal folklore, customs and rituals still exists – in the form of ceremonies, clothing worn/uniforms and behaviour expected of members. In order to become a member of a distinct group, the individual may have to embrace any or all of these – to become 'one of the boys/girls' in order to be accepted. Fitting into the group, an organised scheme of things, gives the individual a sense of identity and sense of belonging.

The last century has also seen the gradual break-up of the class system. Advertisers, for instance, now no longer target customers by social class or income group, but do a "Values and Lifestyle Analysis". They identify 'social tribes' and their characteristic features according to tastes, aspirations, values and particular lifestyle.

Project: Values and Lifestyle Analysis

(a) Are you aware of your 'social tribe'? Try writing up your own Values and Lifestyle Analysis to determine where you think you fit in to today's society, using as guidelines the tastes, aspirations, values and lifestyle list mentioned above. Or are you an aspiring drop-out? If so, what social tribe did you drop out from, and why?

(b) Have you ever belonged to a 'gang'? Has there ever been a particular group to which you aspired to belong, perhaps dressing in accordance with their adopted style or behaving like them? Or are you at present a member of a particular organisation, perhaps with a recognised constitution and regular meetings? How do you feel/did you feel as a group member – are you/were you happy in the organisation, did it give you a feeling of security, did you 'fit in'? Or have you reached the conclusion that you're better off as a loner not belonging to any group?

(c) Aggression and War: one of the basic features of tribalism is the support given which allows a group of individuals both to defend themselves more successfully than one person alone, but also to expand their territory. There is safety in numbers – but also the potential to spread oneself, one's lifestyle and thinking, and impose these on others. One skinhead alone on a train may not be perceived as a threat to other passengers – six skinheads is a different matter, even though their behaviour may be totally innocuous. Appearances alone may be enough to present an aggressive front. Have you any prejudices like this about a particular group of people that you perceive as a threat? Can you analyse how they came about? Relate in writing any aggressive incidents, either experienced by you or heard about, that have caused you to regard this group in this way. Try to put yourself in their shoes and examine their reasons for their aggression: frustration? Feelings of inferiority? Or are they just being pig-headed?

6. *Positive Thinking*
   Shantideva was an eighth century Indian master of Mahayana Buddhism. He has this to advise:

   > *"If you can solve your problem,*
   > *Then what is the need of worrying?*
   > *If you cannot solve it,*
   > *Then what is the use of worrying?"*

We waste an enormous amount of energy on negatives such as hatred, anger, frustration and grief, which would be far better employed for positive ends. First, however, we need to recognise them for what they are and identify the source of the trouble, before making a conscious effort to eliminate the root cause. And the source of the trouble will probably be found deep within ourselves: we may try to place the blame for our misfortunes elsewhere and this will give temporary respite – we may feel quite good about ourselves for a while. But the serious problems will require a serious change of attitude to enable positive thinking.

(a) *"A Wish-fulfilling Treasure Vase"*: imagine a large oriental vase emitting clouds of fragrant smoke. It burns all our impurities, defects and defilements. What are your 'impurities, defects and defilements' that you'd like to be rid of? What do you think would make you a better person? Either make a list, or choose one particular thing, and explain to the 'vase' why it should grant you this wish. This could take the form of a poem, as in Keats' *Ode on a Grecian Urn*, or a conversation in which the vase asks you questions before granting your wish.

(b) *"Growing Pains"*: these don't finish when we leave teenager-dom! They continue throughout life, as we develop into more mature people. What growing pains have you experienced in adult life, and what have they taught you? What ploys did you use to overcome them? Are you still a rebel against author-ity, for instance, or still blaming your parents for emotional problems even though you may now be a parent yourself? Have you been able to use your own growing-up experiences postitively, to ensure that history doesn't repeat itself from generation to generation? Assume you're on the psychia-trist's couch and explain to him/her past growing pains, and any you're still undergoing.

(c) *Purging Memories*:

> *"If you are upset by a stinging memory that persists, such as a negative incident at work, first see in your mind an image of the situation or the people involved, but without negative judgement or resistance."*
>
> Tulku Thondup in *The Healing Power of the Mind*.

Try looking at it from their point of view: can you at least understand where they're coming from, even if you don't agree with it at all? Try writing the same incident from *both* points of view – yours and the person who's upset you. Try to put your-self into the mind and thinking of the other person, define their motives and explain them, and then do the same for yourself. "He who sees both sides of a problem sees nothing at all"? – Are you now any wiser for having looked at both viewpoints, or not?

7. *Sources of Inspiration*

(a) *Daylight*: we associate darkness with sadness, depression, pain. Daylight, and especially sunshine, on the other hand, have the opposite effect and can brighten the spirits and give energy to humans as well as plants. Observe one particular view or scene at different times of day, as the light changes, and describe how your impressions, and feelings about the scene, change with the light variations.

(b) *Artificial Light*: candles now tend to be associated with a reli-gious setting, floodlights have sporting connotations and we even have sun-lamps to fake sunshine and give us a sun-tan. Describe a source of artificial light that you're familiar with, the quality of light that it gives out (e.g. the flickering effect of candles in a church), and compare it with 'the real thing' for providing feel-good factor. Have you any memories associated with lighting – a child's nite-lite by the bed, for instance – or its opposite, being afraid of the dark?

(c) *Light as Symbol*: we use several metaphorical phrases associated with light in everyday speech, e.g. 'daylight dawning' (for truth); 'a ray of sunshine' (for the relief of depression); 'let the sun shine in' (to relieve sadness); 'the cold light of day' (what dawns when all the euphoria and emotions are over and done with); 'in broad daylight/daylight robbery' (blatant and open theft or cheating). Can you use one of these phrases as the subject of a short prose piece to demonstrate its metaphorical use? For instance, have you watched 'daylight dawning' on someone's face as truth is recognised? Or has it happened to you – and what did it feel like? Was it a cold grey dawn as something unpleasant was realised – or glorious sunlight entering the brain?

(d) *"A Weight Off My Mind"*: we use weight as a metaphor for the mental burdens we carry, – worries that can weigh us down, or guilt. The following ideas use weight symbolically to represent problems people are going to have to face. Describe a young man or woman who is concerned with his/her bodyweight to the extent of being obsessive about it – either anorexic, or determined that 'big is beautiful' and they're going to stay that way. Imagine a situation that might turn these feelings around: the realisation dawns that he/she won't get on in life thinking that way and that relationships won't flourish. Perhaps this is due to something someone he/she respects or loves has said; a conversation overheard; an incident in public life (e.g. a pop or TV star has to undergo treatment for the same thing). Write this person's diary entry – talking to themselves on paper – where the decision is made to re-think the weight attitude, and he/she is telling him/herself officially that this will be the course of future action.

(e) *Weight-Lifting*: weight-training sessions are a diversion for one young man from facing up to the fact that he's having trouble keeping a girlfriend for any length of time. He's assuming that girls will fall for those muscles, so all he has to do is put in sufficient time at the gym. The moment of truth comes when he overhears his current girlfriend talking to another female friend of hers, complaining about the amount of time he weight-trains and what the resulting physique looks like. Write the girls' conversation, then in prose narrative describe his feelings and thoughts as a result of what he's overheard.

(f) *The Human Voice*: is there a particular type of voice that always annoys you? Perhaps it may be because it's high-pitched, or breathless; or it could be due to the particular accent – either regional, or a strong foreign accent. Can you think why you find this type of voice annoying? Was there someone who spoke like this whom you hated – and therefore you always associate this type of voice with hateful people, as soon as they open their mouths? Or is it regional/social prejudice, against people from a particular part of the country, or a particular social stratum? How did that prejudice come about? Describe the type of voice and what it is that you dislike about it. Does it grate on the ear, for instance, or make you want to interrupt the person to help them 'get it out' if there's a slight speech impediment (e.g. a lisp or stutter)?

(g) *Your Own Voice*: the annoying voice referred to in (f) above could even be your own! If so, what is it about your own voice that annoys you – delivery, perhaps? Would you like to be able to stand up and make a spontaneous speech to a crowd of people, but haven't the confidence? If not, why not? Lack of confidence in your vocabulary, for instance? Or is it that you've inherited a local accent or way of talking that you wish you hadn't? Describe your feelings about your own voice.

(h) *Singing*: do you enjoy singing yourself, or is it something you never do? Is it a form of release for you – either to express faith or emotion, or simply 'make a noise'? Whose singing do you admire – either one particular singer or a *type* of singing? What is it that appeals to you about this one singer or type of singing? Consider the whole range of types of singing, from hymns to reggae, folk songs to opera. Then describe it as if to someone who is not at all familiar with it, and explain why you find it particularly appealing.

8. *Herbal Remedies*

Theophrastus Bombastus von Hohenheim, born in 1493, is far better known by his adopted nickname Paracelsus. He was the first alchemist to suggest the production from plants of medicines that heal. Today there has been a revived interest in the long tradition of herbal remedies begun by Paracelsus, since the modern medical profession is increasingly seen as drug dispensers rather than healers. Herbalists, on the other hand, don't wait until someone is already ill before trying to heal them, but use herbs as a part of everyday diet to ward off possible disease – prevention rather than cure.

Can you think of a herb or spice that would suit you, to heal any of your physical or mental ailments? If you aren't familiar enough with herbal remedies in existence, make one up as a cure-all. Now write a short story in which this same herbal remedy is used by someone else successfully, working as you think it would work for you. This could be present-day, or in the past, e.g. a medieval herbalist prescribes this remedy. Does it work in the nick of time, for instance (thus preventing someone being burnt as a witch)? In choosing your herbal remedy, ask yourself:

- What does its smell remind me of?
- What does its taste remind me of?
- What dishes do I associate with it?
- What does its appearance remind me of?
- Any incidents or anecdotes associated with it?
- Any people associated with it?
- Can I use it as a symbol (e.g. chilli peppers for someone who is 'red-hot' sexually?)
- Any interesting history associated with it?

9. *Deities and Demons*

(a) If you were a deity, what would you wish to do/how would you wish to behave to improve life on earth? What *sort* of deity would you want to be – anonymous and in the background, doing good works, or regularly worshipped (and if so, *how* would you want to be worshipped?) Make a list of items you'd want to put right, then write your Declaration of Intent as if presenting it to be read by those interviewing you for the job of deity.

(b) So you're now a fully paid-up deity, and you encounter *your first demon*. What does this demon represent? (e.g. laziness; greed). How are you going to sort him/her/it out? (Does it have a gender?) What does this demon look like – an agglomeration of all the appearance traits you most dislike in humans? Design your demon in writing, then sort it out: this could take the form of a persuasive discourse as if a politician is talking, trying to be diplomatic, or a St. George and the Dragon encounter with you swinging your sword. Or both – if diplomacy fails your only alternative may be violence. But have a good think as to what would be most effective in the long-term and which method you'd feel best about afterwards. Now describe your actions in prose as if for a science fiction story.

10. *Fairy Tales*
Want to vent your spleen regarding your mother-in-law? Write a fairy tale – with her as the wicked witch! Got a phobia about something? Personify it as the monster of your fairy-tale! Fairy tales are an excellent outlet for whatever's troubling you: you can safely disguise a person or a feeling within a weird or grotesque tale (even a humorous one), and give them their comeuppance. Ask yourself the following questions and make notes accordingly, to get you started:

• If the 'baddy' of your fairy tale is based on human characteristics, what is the *outstanding feature* to be, e.g. greed? Slovenliness? Jealously?

- What *physical form* would this outstanding feature take? Is greed best personified by someone grossly overweight, and slovenliness by a dirty, smelly, long-haired monster? Have you any drawings, or photos of someone in stage costume, that you can use to work from, which just typify for you what you expect someone with such a character to look like?
- Is there *one particular detail* of your baddy's appearance you can use as a symbol for their main character feature, e.g. long fingernails for someone grasping who digs in possessively and won't let go; fangs for someone who spits venom and hatred all the time?
- *Storyline*: there are many 'standard' fairy-tale motifs that you can re-use for your updated, modern version, e.g. a girl in a deep sleep; a man who has been changed into a monster and only a kiss from a beautiful girl will release him; a large bird kidnapping a baby; children lost in a dark wood; the retrieval of an object (cf. no. 3 in this chapter: Symbols); forbidden or magic fruit; the elixir of life. Can you take one of these as your storyline and translate it to the present-day? Set your hero or heroine a task to be performed or a goal to be aimed at.
- *Setting*: caves and castles feature often in fairy-tales, as do deep, dark woods and magic mountains. Decide on your terrain: is this to be an 'urban' fairy-tale? A multi-storey block that continues up to heaven indefinitely? Is your monster the personification of a bad driver, wreaking havoc in traffic?
- *Hero/heroine description*: does she have yards of long hair that refuses to stop growing at a rate of knots? Does he use his sword as a phallic symbol, thrusting at all and sundry, or wear his armour as a shield to hide from the world? Your hero or heroine will have some such personal problem, e.g. the gaining of confidence to stand up for him/herself, which your fairy-tale will work out for them – always remembering that a fairy-tale needs a happy ending!

11. *Get Thee to a Nunnery*
    The idea of a 'retreat' – whether for religious contemplation, or the 'refuge' variety to escape the world for whatever reason, is something we probably all think we could do with at some time

in our lives. People need time and space without the hassle of other work demands, other people, other pressures. The chance to stand back and assess the significance of events – or simply to 'get away from it all' – is something we humans need from time to time. For some this may simply be thinking time; for others, a chance to talk about problems with someone who isn't involved and who can offer impartial advice.

Writing – e.g. a diary – can supply this escape/refuge on the page even if the physical world can't fit it in (as in actually visiting a refuge/retreat). But imagine you were able to make such an escape to a retreat: what would you choose to discuss and write about? Suppose you have the opportunity, free from all constraints such as job or family, to unburden yourself at leisure and purge the soul. What topics would you want to cover? Has your religious conviction (or lack of it), for instance, always been nagging away at the back of your mind? Do you carry the burden of guilt about something? Is there anything like that, which you've always been meaning to sort out mentally, but somehow never got round to it? Try to think yourself into the peace and undisturbed quiet of a retreat, then write about how you would use this opportunity to try and solve any mental problems (if you've already visited a retreat, describe what you found there and your experiences).

12. *Working from Quotes*
    Choose at least one of the following selection of quotes to write about, in the form of a 'discussion paper'. That means you will need to examine both sides of the argument (if there is one), or all aspects of the topic, as if a discussion were taking place between two people of differing views/backgrounds/attitudes. It may help to make lists 'for' and 'against' first, or to do a brainstorm and jot down any ideas that occur in connection with the topic (you may well then find you have to ask yourself *why* those ideas occurred to you). Summarise what you're going to say in your first paragraph, then work through your discussion paragraph by paragraph, then try to draw an overall conclusion in your last paragraph. If you can't come to any definite conclusion, say so – and explain why!

    • "Religion: morality heightened by emotion?"

- "It is easier to devote one's life to fanaticism than to liberalism."
- "Love does not come at the beginning of a relationship, but at its end. It is the reward of a shared experience, the usual irritations and commitment."
- "It is easier to be depressed or aggressive than patiently to work through a problem and solve it."
- "Religion has a habit of telling you where you ought to be and not starting from where you are."
- "Being a husband is a whole-time job. That is why so many husbands fail. They cannot give their entire attention to it." (Arnold Bennett)
- "Sweet is revenge – especially to women." (Lord Byron)

13. *Attitudes to Writing*

    How did you feel about writing before you began this book? Has your attitude altered in any way? If so, how? What have you observed about other people's attitudes to writing and writers? Do they believe it's a dying art, as technology takes over in the workplace, for instance? Answer these questions in note form, then expand your notes into a piece of prose 300–500 words long.

10 Case studies

THE HYPOTHETICAL CASES DESCRIBED IN THIS chapter allow you to do two things: to sit in the psychiatrist's chair and listen to someone else's problems, then offer possible solutions; and to continue each story beyond the details given, using fictional writing to answer the question "what happens next?" There may be several possible outcomes, conflicting advice you'll have to choose from and various courses of action that could be recommended to solve the dilemma posed. As with any effective writing, you will have to put yourself into the mind of the characters outlined, and try to sympathise with each one or at least understand their behaviour and motives. You may find yourself in some cases immediately siding with one viewpoint and a course of action will be clear-cut. In other cases, there may be no right or wrong and a diplomatic solution will have to be found – in which case, your resulting writing will have to point this out.

1. You enter the small private office of a work colleague and on talking to her become immediately aware that she's been drinking heavily. This is the third time in as many weeks: you've known her many years and the last time it happened you had a chat with her, suggested she go straight home, and you agreed to sign her off sick. She swore that it wouldn't happen again, she would sort out her problems, and she thanked you profusely for covering for her. This time, as soon as she realises you know she's been drinking, she bursts into tears. Describe your response:

   - Do you put your arms round her and offer comfort – a shoulder to cry on?
   - Do you become extremely angry and give her a good telling-off?
   - Do you turn on your heel and leave the room, hoping she'll sober up quickly?
   - Do you loiter tentatively at a distance, in embarrassment?

Your own motives will play a part in your response: do you sympathise, knowing what tremendous pressure she's been under recently, or do you want to see the back of her, even though you've always got on reasonably well? Following writing up your immediate on-the-spot response to the situation, decide what happens next. What are the possible outcomes, which outcome is preferable from your point of view, her point of view – and for the office as a whole? If this were a scene in a television soap opera and you were the writer – where would you take the plot from here? Work out at least one possible storyline in note form, then write up the next scene in dialogue.

2. *What Happened Before?* In this case, you will need to work out not only what happens next, but what happened first to cause the following scenario:

One day you answer your doorbell to find your next-door neighbour on your doorstep apoplectic with anger. He pushes you aside, bursts in and attacks your partner with his fists. You have no idea what he/she has done to deserve this, but a wild stream of possible answers races through your brain: has the dog made a mess on his front lawn again? Was it the smoke from that bonfire drifting across his garden that's tipped him over the edge? Has your partner parked half across his driveway again, so that he can't get his car out? Or is there something far more sinister in this, something you know nothing about?

Decide first what the cause has been – something sufficient to create such a build-up of venom on the part of your neighbour. What sort of person is likely to respond like this? Draw a character sketch in writing of the neighbour, leading to his motive for the violent attack. Then decide what happens next: do you step in wielding a shovel and knock him out, grab the phone and dial 999, – or run?

Having looked at the scenario from the onlooker's point of view, next assume you are the attacker, and argue his case in a written statement made to the police. Would such a response ever be justified – was it a last resort where all else had failed? And how to resolve this animosity – where to from here? Write your lawyer's response, offering advice and suggestions for an agreeable outcome.

3. John's girlfriend, Sue, had gone out on Saturday night with another man. He was looking forward to seeing her as usual, and when he discovered he'd been 'stood up' he was not only shocked, but felt betrayed and very angry. He armed himself with a flick-knife and visited various pubs until he found the pair of them, then attacked them both. The police were called and John ended up in a prison cell, doing time for GBH. Later, Sue decided to write him a 'Dear John' letter, hoping to break off relations once and for all. He wrote back accusingly and threateningly. Consider *both* points of view, then write both letters – these may contain accusations, slander and insults, or perhaps contrition and apologies (how would *you* feel if you were either of them?) Whichever style you choose, try to convey their emotions realistically.

4. *"A Complete Break"*: Jane had finally made up her mind: time to walk away. Time to stop the clock, cut off the telephone … she didn't *have* to lead this life. Not *her* life at all, but the life her mother had wanted for her, her boss and her boyfriend now expected of her. How many people would it really affect if she just packed her bags and walked out? And would they even notice she'd gone?…

   (a) Continue Jane's thought-processes as she decides to leave her job, the area she's living in, and everything that so far has added up to her not feeling happy. She needs to justify the move to herself and summon up the determination. Has she a new job to apply for, is she thinking of going on a residential course or going to stay with a friend some distance away – or sticking a pack on her back and travelling for a year or two?

   (b) When you've examined her thoughts, look at the situation from *her mother's point of view* – her reactions to Jane's leaving, the questions she would ask (of Jane and of herself), and her worries.

   (c) *How does the boyfriend react*? Is it a case of "What did I do to deserve this treatment?" or "The ungrateful bitch – glad I'm rid of her"? Or does he go round and try to find her to beat her up? Decide on his reactions, then write his conversation with a male friend explaining what's happened to

137

Jane. Is he going to bluster his way out of any blame, try and pretend he's not hurt, or rant and rave in anger?

5. *"In the Psychotherapist's Chair"*: A middle-aged man has been left by his wife and two children; he has counselling and/or psychotherapy. As his therapist, you discover his parents had let him down when he was a child, by making promises they didn't keep, forgetting his birthday, etc. and his way of coping was to learn not to trust them – or anyone else. So he never really trusted his wife, he was irrationally jealous, and she'd had enough. She was by now back at work, and doing well in her job – something he was also jealous about as his own career appeared to be going nowhere. What would your advice be to this man? Can you advise him how to rebuild his life (both mentally and practically)?

   After several sessions he starts making excuses about the times of sessions – he can't make certain times per week, so you adjust to his needs. Then he can't manage this new session arrangement, and expresses resentment to you, for not meeting *his* needs, not really caring about him, and 'being just like the rest' (i.e. not trustworthy). How do you react? What would you write up in your case study notes at this point?

6. A woman recently turned 50, married 26 years, is suffering from 'empty nest' syndrome as her youngest child leaves home. She hasn't had a career, having been married to a domineering, chauvinistic husband who believed that home and children were a woman's domain and that he was 'giving her everything she needed'. Only now has she come to realise that her dependence on her husband and their marriage is totally stifling and that she has many years ahead of her with nothing satisfying to do. She decides to begin an Open University degree course. When her husband discovers her intentions, he hits the roof (is he afraid she may outstrip him brain-wise? Will a degree for her undermine his dominance?) She realises the only way for her to achieve any personal advancement will be to divorce him, and begins proceedings despite his recriminations and the criticism of neighbours.

   Using diary format, write down her thoughts as she goes through this painful decision-making process: can you imagine how she's feeling? Then write down *his* thoughts and reactions when it finally dawns that 'she means it' and he is first informed that divorce proceedings are underway.

7. Jake is 12 when his mother dies from a drugs overdose. He hasn't seen his father since he was 8, when his father abandoned the two of them. They manage to trace his father, who agrees to accept responsibility for Jake, and is on his way to the temporary foster home Jake is now living in, to collect him. But the boy doesn't trust this man who abandoned him and his mother, has had enough of Social Services, and decides to quit. He takes all the money he can lay his hands on, and catches the train to London, intending to live on the streets if necessary.

You have a three-hour train journey sitting next to Jake, and get talking. What is your advice to him? Should he give his father the benefit of the doubt and try to make a go of it? Where would he prefer to live? What about schooling, etc.? Write the ensuing dialogue showing how you'd go about discovering his past, his intentions, and then reasoning with him. Jake's responses may well include argument, surprise, and rejection of all your suggestions.

8. You have new neighbours next door. In the recent fine weather you've been spending time out in your garden, but your enjoyment has been spoiled by what's coming over the hedge: loud, persistent swearing, apparently between both husband and wife and father and son.

(a) Decide what it is that annoys you most – the noise level (would the annoyance be the same if the sound were music?); is it the actual swearing you object to? Or the interpersonal abuse? Work out your reasons, then put your complaint in writing to them.

(b) You are the teacher of an 8 year old whose behaviour in school is disruptive, mainly due to his language – persistent swearing and abuse directed at teachers. What is your strategy going to be to prevent this (short of excluding him from school)? You meet with his parents, who turn out to be persistent swearers themselves. There is no improvement, so you write your confidential report for the eyes of the head teacher and school governors, explaining the situation and any possible solutions you can suggest.

9. *Telephone Calls*

   (a) You start to receive abusive telephone calls at odd times of the day and night, which you report to the police. Meanwhile how do you respond to what is coming over the phone when you lift the receiver? Write the dialogue of one abusive call with more than one possible response on your part, e.g. you respond light-heartedly, treating it as a joke; you give as good as you get, trying to frighten off the caller; you pretend you're someone else – a foreigner/an alien/someone mentally deranged (and how does your abusive caller then respond?)

   (b) Make your own abusive phone call! Decide who you'd really like to 'have a go' at; then decide the tone you're going to adopt – sarcastic, humorous, just plain nasty? Write your side of the dialogue (you can assume the person at the other end won't be able to get a word in edgeways).

   (c) Someone has mistaken your phone number for the Samaritans helpline, and you find yourself having a conversation with a person who is suicidal. How will you go about this? You're afraid that if you ring off, it could tip your caller over the edge, whereas if you continue to talk you may just be able to help. Work out the points of view of both persons and their reasoning, then write the ensuing dialogue. One of the most difficult things about this piece of writing will probably be: where to finish? Does one of you put the phone down? Or can the situation be saved by someone else turning up at your caller's end?

10. *Anorexia*: Amanda is a highly intelligent 16 year old who has become increasingly weight-conscious. She has started refusing to eat school meals, so her mother has been giving her packed lunches, but she's throwing them away. She's also started taking laxatives at night, and whenever she has 'put on a show' and eaten a meal with the family, she's promptly vomited it up again afterwards. As a result, her bodyweight has dropped to six stone and she's become a skeleton.

Her mother is at her wits end, but assumes the only way to treat Amanda is to *make* her eat. Only when school steps in and suggests Amanda see a psychiatrist do they start to get to the bottom of things. As Amanda points out to her psychiatrist, she's never really discussed her eating disorder with her mother, and she doesn't feel her mother has really ever tried to understand.

(a) The psychiatrist arranges for both Amanda and her mother to come in and discuss the problem on 'neutral ground' at the hospital. The resulting confrontation throws a lot of light on the reasons for Amanda's anorexia. Work out what you think these might be, then write the three-way conversation, with Amanda accusing and her mother on the defensive, and the psychiatrist asking probing questions in between.

(b) Her mother is writing a letter to her sister in Australia, telling her of the recent upheavals. Write the letter from the mother's viewpoint – this could be asking for advice, having a good moan, or self-examination and questioning on the page.

(c) Have you always been happy with your appearance, or hated it? Ever tried to alter it drastically, or abused your body in any way? Describe your motives, what you did, other people's reactions, and the outcome. What would your advice be to Amanda, or any other teenage girl like her?

11. One of your parents, or an elderly relative or older close friend, has been admitted to hospital as a long-stay patient. There is every possibility they may not recover sufficiently to be released. He/she is a gregarious type who has always had a good social life, and being a member of a large family has always been surrounded by frequent visitors. The long hours on the ward till visiting time are proving very frustrating – reading has become difficult – and he/she is becoming a nuisance for others on the ward, wanting to talk all the time even when they're resting or wanting to mind their own business.

You offer to become a 'scribe' to write down his/her memoirs when you visit, and this offer is eagerly taken up. Unfortunately, you get far more then you bargained for: all sorts of skeletons appear from the family closet, described with gossipy relish.

How do you respond? Do you note everything down, only to 'edit' it for family consumption later (without telling your relative/friend)? Or try to suggest alternative content for the memoirs – if so, how do you go about this? You wish to remain on good terms with this person for what time they have left alive, and don't want to hurt or alienate them – and they are obviously enjoying telling you such details, unaware of the embarrassment they are causing you. Suggest at least one possible way out of this dilemma – more if you can.

12. *Kidnapping*: a childless couple, Diana and Jim, have tried every method available over the years in order to conceive, but have been unsuccessful. Now aged 36, Diana is depressed and desperate, obsessed with her need for a child. She is even becoming alienated from Jim, who suggested she seek psychiatric help – but all that led to was an almighty row. Out shopping one day in her local shopping precinct, Diana finds a pram left unattended outside a shop, with the baby inside it crying. She bends over to offer comfort …

    That evening Jim returns home from work to discover Diana sitting nursing a beautiful baby. Relate:

    • The thoughts going through Diana's mind as she 'kidnaps' someone else's child;
    • Jim's reaction on discovering what she's done, and the ensuing words between them (in dialogue form): is he furious/horrified/comforting?
    • Describe the real mother's reaction when she discovers her baby has been stolen;
    • What is Diana's mother's reaction, when she comes to visit that day and finds a baby has appeared? Relate the conversation between them as her mother tries to offer counselling and Diana tries to explain/justify her actions.

13. When Kerry was seven, her mother's behaviour began to change. The house became increasingly untidy, food wasn't forthcoming for her and her sister, there were tantrums, a smashed mirror, the kitchen wrecked on one occasion. Kerry returned home from school one day to find her mother had tried to dye her hair bright red, without much success. The result was so

horrific that Kerry showed her fear of this 'harridan' – and her mother reacted by threatening her with the big kitchen knife, a weapon that continued to be the ultimate threat for the rest of her childhood, and featured centrally in her resulting nightmares. Her mother's nervous breakdown meant she had to be hospitalised. Her parents then divorced, her mother re-married, and her stepfather proved rather too keen to 'put the girls to bed', threatening violence if they told anyone he'd been touching them. Only later in life during therapy did Kerry become fully aware of what she had suffered – sexual abuse and the threat of violence. In the meantime, she had suppressed these memories, and was having enormous trouble entering any sexual relationship.

(a) Can you put forward any possible reasons for her mother's nervous breakdown? Why do you think she reacted the way she did, when threatening a seven year old with a knife? Was this just a knee-jerk reaction? Having thought through what might cause a mother to react this way, write the (brief) dialogue that may well have taken place between Kerry and her mother during the confrontation.

(b) Kerry's experiences as a child have resulted in a phobia about knives. Describe a kitchen scene where Kerry (now an adult), having bottled up her fears for years but always having been 'funny about knives', reacts to a female flat-mate who is fooling around with one. How do you think she'd behave? Will she now feel able to unburden herself of past fears and try to explain truthfully why she feels that way about knives – or will there be endless excuses/explanations to try and prevent her flat-mate's questions?

(c) Kerry, at 16, is seriously interested in a boy, who wants to begin a sexual relationship, but she feels unable to go ahead. Just having him touch her brings back all sorts of horrific memories – and he's becoming increasingly frustrated. Her only reaction is to insist that she 'can't explain', but this only leads to a row. Write Kerry's diary entry on the day after the row, in which she's asking herself all sorts of questions, not least of all "where do I go from here?"

143

14. *Bereavement*: Wendy, who is in her thirties, lost her father six months ago. While still having to cope with her own grief, she now has the added problem of her mother, who was virtually numb immediately after the death and until the funeral was over. Only after that did her mother enter a real stage of mourning. Even now, six months later, she is 'refusing to get on with life' – not taking care of herself, hardly ever going out of her bungalow, not bothering to eat properly – in short, she has retired from the world. Wendy is finding her mother's reaction almost as painful to cope with as her father's death; she wants to offer comfort, but nothing seems to help.

(a) What would your advice be to Wendy? What approaches can you think of that may help to bring her mother out of this torpid state? Make notes about possible solutions.

(b) Have you any similar experiences from real life? Relate the details in narrative form.

15. *Disability*

(a) Eric and Emily Jones have a daughter, Christine, who suffers from spina bifida. Up to the age of eight, Christine had attended their local school in her wheelchair and was happily integrated with the rest of the pupils. She had many friends and was making excellent progress educationally. Then the previous headmistress retired and a new one took over who had just moved into the area. The new head, Mrs. Bryson, was not 'wheelchair friendly', to use Emily's description. The Jones' had to do continuous battle from then on to have their daughter treated equally and included in all school activities as she had been in the past, simply because of one person's attitude. They didn't want to have to move Christine from this school, as she was totally familiar with it and had coped so well in the past. Emily Jones decides to write an official letter to Mrs. Bryson, plus a copy to the chairman of the school's governors, complaining about the difference in attitude and the effect it's having on their daughter. She also intends to write a short article for a local magazine. She doesn't hold out much hope for an overnight sea-change in the new head's attitude, but feels she should at least register a protest, and in writing things down releases some of her own angst. Assume you are Emily Jones, and write her letter, then do a 300 word magazine article relating the situation.

(b) Kelly is in her thirties and is wheelchair-bound. She has applied for a university place to read English, and her interview is pending. She enquires over the telephone regarding wheelchair access to the English Department building, and is assured there is access and a lift to the rear. Kelly and her partner arrive in good time and discover the 'tradesman's entrance', as it becomes known by Kelly, up an alleyway at the far back of the building. The door is locked and no one is around to let them in. As it begins to pour with rain, her partner goes in search of help and Kelly is left in her wheelchair outside the building getting soaked.

Eventually a porter with a key is found and Kelly's wheelchair just fits into the small service lift. Understandably, Kelly enters her interview furious at this standard of provision for the disabled, and determines that after her interview she will make as much fuss as possible – shout it from the rooftops if necessary – to improve access. She is accepted for a place, and on further investigation she discovers that this rear alleyway is her *only* way into the building – i.e. the only way of escape for wheelchairs in case of fire. She begins a campaign to bring wheelchair access up to the standard required by law, but finds this appears to be a low priority in the university's budget. For Kelly, 'shouting it from the rooftops' begins with letter-writing. Can you write three separate letters, as if you were Kelly in her wheelchair, to the following:

- Her local MP
- The university chancellor's office
- A letter for publication in the university's student magazine

You may need to alter content and tone slightly, depending on who will be reading the letter, but your main aim will be to publicise the plight of anyone who needs good, permanently available, wheelchair access.

Write yourself well book list

You may find any of the following of interest in helping you to start writing, for the creation of ideas, and for further understanding of how writing can heal:

ARNOLD: Roslyn, 1991 *Writing Development – Magic in the Brain*, OUP, Oxford.

BENSON: Judi, and FALK: Agneta, (eds.), 1996 *The Long Pale Corridor – Contemporary Poems of Bereavement*, Bloodaxe, London.

BION: W. R., 1961 *Experiences in Groups*, Basic Books, New York.

BLUE: Lionel, 1979 *A Backdoor to Heaven – An Autobiography*, Collins, London.

BROWN: Daniel, 1997 *Principles of Art Therapies*, Harper Collins, London.

COOPER: Judy, and LEWIS: Jenny, 1995 *Who Can I Talk To? – The User's Guide to Therapy and Counseling*, Hodder and Stoughton, London.

DE BONO: Edward, 1970 *Lateral Thinking*, Penguin, London.

DE QUINCEY: Thomas, 1822 *Confessions of an English Opium Eater*, see www.lycaeum.org

DOUGLAS: T., 1995 *Survival in Groups: The Basics of Group Membership*, OUP, Oxford.

GERSIE: Alida, and KING: Nancy, 1990 *Storymaking in Education and Therapy*, JKP, London.

GREENBERG: Sheldon, and ORTIZ: Elisabeth Lambert, 1983 *The Spice of Life*, Michael Joseph, London.

GROSS: R.D., 1987 Psychology: *The Science of Mind and Behaviour*, Hooder and Stoughton, London.

HARTLEY: Peter, 1997 *Group Communication,* Routledge, London.

HAY: Louise, 1988 *You Can Heal Your Life,* Eden Grove Editions, London.

HILL: Selima, 1989 *The Accumulation of Small Acts of Kindness,* Chatto and Windus, London.

JONES: M., 1953 *The Therapeutic Community,* Basic Books, New York.

KNIGHT: Lindsay, 1986 *Talking to a Stranger – A Guide to Psychotherapy,* Hodder and Stoughton, London.

LEVETE: Gina, 1993 *Letting Go of Loneliness,* Element Books, London.

METCALF: C. W., and FELIBLE: Roma, 1992 *Lighten Up: Survival Skills for People Under Pressure,* Addison-Wesley, USA.

MORRIS: Desmond, and MARSH: Peter, 1988 *Tribes,* Pyramid, London.

MURPHY: Gardner, 1958 *Human Potentialities,* Basic Books, New York.

NAWE: 1996 *Creative Writing in Special Education,* NAWE, York.

PARKER: Rennie, 2007 *Starting to Write,* Studymates, Abergele.

PECK: M. Scott, 1978 *The Road Less Traveled,* Simon and Schuster, New York.

PENNEBAKER: James: *Opening Up: The Healing Power of Expressing Emotions,* Guilford Press, New York.

POSTHUMA: Barbara, 1996 *Small Groups in Counselling and Therapy,* Allyn and Bacon (2nd ed.), USA.

RANKIN-BOX: Denise, 1995 *The Nurses Handbook of Complementary Therapies,* Churchill Livingstone, London.

RICE: J., SAUNDERS: C., O'SULLIVAN: T. and ROBERSON: S., 1996 *Successful Group Work: A Practical Guide for Students in Further and Higher Education,* Kogan Page, London.

ROGERS: Carl, 1970 *Encounter Groups,* Harper and Row, New York.

SAIL: Lawrence, (ed.), 1988 *First and Always,* Faber and Faber, London.

SCHNEIDER: Myra, and KILLICK: John, 1998 *Writing for Self-discovery,* Element Books, London.

STEVENS: Anthony, 1995 *Private Myths,* Penguin, London.

THONDUP: Tulku, 1996 *The Healing Power of the Mind,* Penguin, London.

THORLEY: L., and GREGORY: R., 1994 *Using Group-based Learning in Higher Education,* Kogan Page, London.

WEEKS: David, 1995 *Eccentrics,* Weidenfeld and Nicholson, London.

WETTON: Steve, 2007 *Choose Happiness: ten steps to put the magic back into your life,* Aber, Publishing, Abergele.

Glossary of terms

allegory: symbolical narration where people represent mankind in general or a particular type, and objects

ambience: the atmosphere surrounding a person or thing

analysis: breaking-down into parts to understand structure

anecdote: a short narrative of an incident of private life

anthology: a choice collection, especially of poetry

assertiveness training: a management method to enable the affirmation of one's rights without encroaching on the rights of others

aural stimulation: sounds providing mental stimulation when received by the ear

autobiography: the writing of one's own life story

behaviour therapy: a means of treatment by training the patient in new behaviour

biography: the writing of someone else's life-story

brainstorming: intensive group discussion where participants are encouraged to contribute ideas 'off the cuff' without prior consideration

caricature: an absurd or ludicrous imitation or version

case study: a study based on the analysis of one or more examples

catharsis: the purging of the effects of pent-up emotions and repressed thoughts by bringing them to the surface of consciousness

character profile: factual data to do with a fictional character as well as opinions, attitudes, and temperament

cliché: anything stereotyped, hackneyed, over-used

confessions: as a literary genre, a form of autobiography in which intimate and/or guilty matters are 'confessed'

confidant(e): a close friend entrusted with secrets

credo: a belief or set of beliefs

critique: a critical review or analysis of a work of literature

culpable: deserving blame

diagnosis: a formal determining description

didactic: intended to teach (sometimes pedantically or dictatorially so)

discourse: speech or language generally; formal laying-out in words

eavesdroppings: 'listening in' to other people's private conversation

elegy: a song of mourning; a poem in serious, pensive or reflective mood

ethnic/ethnicity: belonging to a particular racial group or cult

extrovert: outgoing, interested in the world outside oneself

faction: fact-based writing with fictional additions

fiction: an invented story

first person: the 'I'-form, the writer speaking for him/herself

free verse: rhythmic verse without constraints such as metre or rhyme

genre: the broad classification of a particular literary style

haiku: a Japanese syllabic verse-form in 3 lines of 5,7,5 syllables, traditionally untitled, and reflecting the human condition

heredity: characteristics transmitted to descendants

hypochondriac: someone suffering from imaginary illness

iambic pentameters: poetry composed in lines of 5 iambs, an iamb being a foot of 2 syllables, short followed by long, or unstressed followed by stressed

illumination: that flash of original inspiration

immersion: becoming totally familiar with all aspects of a topic

incident: a minor event showing hostility and threatening more serious trouble

incubation: letting ideas mature and allowing conjecture

inhibition: restraining action of the unconscious will

introspective: inward-looking; observing and analysing one's own mind

introvert: someone interested mainly in his or her own inner states rather than the outside world

lateral thinking: thinking which does not proceed logically from A to B but adopts new ways of looking at a problem

limerick: a humorous poem of 5 lines with a syllable-count of 9,9,6,6,9 or 10,10,7,7,10 and a rhyme-scheme of a,a,b,b,a

lyrical/lyricism: song-like; expressing private emotion

memoirs: auto/biographical sketches or records

metaphor: something or someone spoken of as actually *being* that which it/they only resemble

metre: the arrangement of poetry lines into a certain number of feet of similar stress

monologue: a speech by one person

narcissist: someone who obtains gratification from self-admiration

narrative/narrator: that part of a literary work which relates events and action (as opposed to dialogue)/the person relating events and action

neurotic: characterised by obsessional fears

non-fiction: purely fact-based

nostalgia: fond remembrance of time past

obituary: a brief account or summary of a deceased person's life

one-to-one: two people either meeting, playing, discussing with, each other

onomatopoeia: the sound of a word echoing or reflecting its sense

optimism: hopefulness; a belief that everything is always for the best

pair-work: the splitting of a class into pairs for each pair to undertake an educational task prior to a plenary session (qv)

palindrome: a word, verse or sentence that reads the same backwards as forwards

palliative: something giving temporary relief, but not a cure

parable: a story told to illustrate some doctrine or moral point

paranoid: suffering from intense, especially irrational, fear or suspicion, or delusions

persona: social façade or public image, very often masking one's inner feelings

perspective: point of view; a way of regarding facts and their relative importance

pessimism: a tendency to always look on the black side of things; despondency

plenary session: the coming together to compare findings after individuals, pairs or small groups have undertaken a task

plot: the working-out of a storyline towards a desired end

poetic licence: an allowable departure from strict fact or truth for the sake of effect

polemic: controversial; a controversial piece of writing or argument

portfolio: a collection of examples of work, e.g. pieces of writing, photographs, paintings, drawings

positive thinking: not worrying about what's gone wrong, but learning from mistakes and using this this knowledge to further our good fortune

preconceived: having an opinion about something prior to actual knowledge of it

premise: details taken as read or events assumed to have occurred prior to the beginning of a plot

prose: language in straightforward sentences and paragraphs

prose poem: a poem set out as prose, apparently in sentences, but using poetic diction

prosody: the study of versification

pseudonym: a fictitious name assumed e.g. by an author

psyche: the soul, spirit or mind; mental and emotional life

psychodrama: a method of treating mental disorders by the patient spontaneously acting out his or her problem

psychopath(ic): (someone) emotionally unstable; pertaining to any disorder of mental functions

rapprochement: an 'approaching' in the sense of people being drawn together

renga: a Japanese form of linked verse where a different poet supplies each verse – either a whole tanka's-worth (qv) or part of one

rhyming couplets: two successive lines of verse that rhyme with each other

saga: a prose narrative often dealing with legends, or family history over several generations

scenario: an outline of how you intend events to shape; a projected sequence of events

scribe: someone to do the actual writing on behalf of an author who dictates

self-disclosure: expressing one's innermost thoughts

side-kick: the assistant or deputy of a literary, TV or film hero/heroine (e.g. Dr. Watson as side-kick to Sherlock Holmes)

simile: a figure of speech where a person or thing is directly compared using 'as … as' or the word 'like'

slant rhyme: indirect rhyme where words do not correspond exactly, e.g. 'seen' and 'born' (as opposed to 'seen' and 'been')

soap opera: TV or radio drama concerning everyday lives of a family or other small group(s), originally sponsored by soap manufacturers

sonnet: a 14-line poem divided into 8 lines stating the theme and then 6 lines offering an explanation or giving an answer, often in iambic pentameters

stereotype: a conventional idea or image, often categorising too simplistically

strong verb: a 'doing' word giving a strong impression of what is happening, e.g. 'crawl' as opposed to 'go slowly'; 'belt along' as opposed to 'go fast'

syllabics: verse based on the counting of syllables rather than stress and metre

symbol: an image or object used to represent something such as a concept, e.g. a rose for love

syntax: grammatical structure in sentences; the order in which we expect to find words to make sense

tanka: Japanese verse of 31 syllables, in 5 lines of 5,7,5,7,7 syllables

therapy: the treatment of a disorder by means other than surgery

'**think-piece**': an article written for a magazine or newspaper designed to make the reader thing (as opposed to straightforward news reporting)

third person: written from the point of view of 'he' or 'she'/your hero or heroine

timbre: sound-quality and atmosphere rather than volume

tirade: a long angry holding-forth by one person

trauma: an emotional shock or injury; its ensuing state

verification: testing a theory to see if it works

vertical thinking: thinking logically in a straight line from A to B to C, as opposed to lateral thinking

visualisation: a therapeutic technique where the sufferer employs all five senses to visualise an object, place or experience that gives great pleasure

writer-in-residence: a writer employed by an organisation for a specific period or project, often grant-aided

Post Script

IF YOU HAVE MANAGED TO GET as far as this in *Write Yourself Well*, you will hopefully be convinced that writing can be therapeutic for you personally. So, now it is up to you. How much do you really want to be well? How much do you want to improve your life? The exercises are all here and are designed to help, but you need to take action. It is the action and the thinking with that action that can change your life for the better, but only you can do it. You have the power within you to become the person you so desire to be, so don't be shy, explore your talent. All you have to do is believe it's worthwhile. Writing isn't a one-off occurrence, but a long continuing process. It is a habit that can be acquired with practice and help, and a very rewarding way of releasing your emotions, recording your thoughts – and even purging your soul?

Whilst this is the end of the book, it is only the start of your journey of self-awareness. So go on, surprise yourself with your writing, and continue to *Write Yourself Well*. Please do let me know how you are getting on, as we will need case studies for the second edition of the book and that could be you, anonymity guaranteed.

I will leave you with these few words.

Water of Life

My glass is half-full:
Why is yours half-empty?
You are 50 years old;
I am 50 years young,
And I look forward
To ripening autumn days.
You look back
To a summer of discontent
And shudder at winter's approach.
Your reflection in this pond
Is disturbed by pebbles

Thrown by others; you grimace.
I see myself more clearly,
And I smile.
I look forward to hearing from you.

Regards,
Ann Coffey.
ann.coffey@aber-publishing.co.uk

Index